DATE DUE

SEP 2006

RIDERS BY NIGHT

Kurt Cardigan was quick with a gun, hot-tempered with his fists, and was known as the slickest horse trader in Tucson. But Cardigan wasn't content with his fame. He wanted a woman.

When Docie Balinett, 'a refined young lady', headed West, it looked like the cowpoke's wish would come true. But when Docie's stage didn't arrive, Cardigan struck out in search. Instead of a 'wife', he caught a rifle slug in his chest. Weak from loss of blood, he stumbled home only to find Docie there struggling in another man's fierce embrace...

Nelson Nye was born in Chicago, Illinois. He was educated in schools in Ohio and Massachusetts and attended the Cincinnati Art Academy. His early journalism experience was writing publicity releases and book reviews for the *Cincinnati Times-Star* and the *Buffalo Evening News*. In 1935 he began working as a ranch hand in Texas and California and became an expert on breeding quarter horses on his own ranch outside Tucson, Arizona. Much of this love for horses can be found in exceptional novels such as *Wild Horse Shorty* and *Blood of Kings*. He published his first Western short story in *Thrilling Western* and his first Western novel in 1936. He continued from then on to write prolifically, both under his own name and the bylines Drake C. Denver and Clem Colt. During the Second World War, he served with the U.S. Army Field Artillery. In 1949–1952 he worked as horse editor for *Texas Livestock Journal*. He was one of the founding members of the Western Writers of America in 1953 and served twice as its president. His first Golden Spur Award from the Western Writers of America came to him for best Western reviewer and critic in 1954. In 1958–1962 he was frontier fiction reviewer for the *New York Times Book Review*. His second Golden Spur came for his novel *Long Run*. His virtues as an author of Western fiction include a tremendous sense of authenticity, an ability to keep the pace of a story from ever lagging, and a fecund inventiveness for plot twists and situations. Some of his finest novels have had off-trail protagonists such as *The Barber of Tubac* and both *Not Grass Alone* and *Strawberry Roan* are notable for their outstanding female characters. His books have sold over 50,000,000 copies worldwide and have been translated into the principal European languages. The *Los Angeles Times* once praised him for his "marvelous lingo, salty humor, and real characters." Above all, a Nye Western possesses a vital energy that is both propulsive and persuasive.

RIDERS BY NIGHT

Nelson Nye

First published by Partridge

This hardback edition 2001
by Chivers Press
by arrangement with
Golden West Literary Agency

ISBN 0 7540 8123 0

British Library Cataloguing in Publication Data available

Printed and bound in Great Britain by
Redwood Books, Trowbridge, Wiltshire

1

ITCH FOR A WOMAN

KURT CARDIGAN, big and riled and intolerant of obstacles, shifted his weight from one boot to the other and wished the goddam stage would get a rattle on. He had wasted two hours in this furnace already and not a dust on the whole damned horizon! Nothing but desert, sky and mountains seen through a shimmering film of heat that curled and crawled off the rough plank walks and broiled above the hoof-tracked street in the blistering glare of the noonday sun.

Tucson!

You could have it!

He was a yellow-haired man in trail grimed clothing with a spatter of dust streaked across granite features. A steel-gray glance that was like chilled lightning snapped from under his sun-bleached brows and considered the view with no leavening of charity. His long solid lips pinched in at the corners and impatience lifted his burly shoulders and swung him about in the stage office doorway. Irritation danced from each clank of his spurs and the high-heeled boots took him back to the counter.

"Butterfield'll have to do better than this or the Goverment'll take the damned mails away from him!"

The agent looked up with tired apology. He brushed damp hair back away from his forehead with fingers that left a smudge of ink in their wake.

"We're not often this late—"

"By God, you're plenty late now!"

"That's a pretty rough stretch between here and El Paso—lot of up-an'-down country around Dragoon Springs. . . . A terrible lot of them Indians—"

"He knew all that when he bid in the contract!"

The agent's cheeks flushed but his eyes fell away from the big man's look and he picked up his pen with a shrug of the

1

shoulders. "I'd hurry it for you if I could, Mister Cardigan."

Cardigan's answer to that was a snort.

He wheeled, turned away, clanking back to the door and again, with his legs firmly planted under him, sent his testy stare over the empty miles that spread, dun and tawny, to the faraway pass that cut through the mountains. That way the stage must come if it *did* come. If it didn't come soon he'd go out there and hunt it—or would he?

He didn't know, by God, whether he would or not! There were times when he thought it couldn't get here quick enough; there were others when he'd get to mullin round in his mind and call himself forty kinds of a fool and wish he could send that damn woman back.

He didn't know, by grab, whether he wanted her or not!

He reckoned a man didn't know his luck when he had it.

Take himself, Kurt Cardigan, a man used to baching it— everything going along fine as silk till he'd got that goddam itching for a woman. He could easy of got him any number of squaws but he just couldn't stomach the stink and the grease of them. He wasn't no durned Mexican! What he wanted was a white woman—and none of your goddam floozies, either!

It was the sight of that nester Rickven's daughter that had got it all started and choused him up this way. He'd been doing all right till he had run into *her*.

He'd been passing their shack a mite early one morning— the old man was away, gone to town or something. He'd been following the creek, it being shorter that way, and had come onto her without a rag on her. She'd been poised on that ledge at the pool by the waterfall. The noisy rush of the water, the pine needles or something . . . he guessed his horse hadn't made much sound. He had sat there, struck dumb, scared to open his mouth even. Plump, she was, and redheaded, with the skin of her body looking white as fresh milk.

When he'd finally woke up he had got the hell out of there.

But he hadn't forgot her. Nor the look of her body with her hands trying to cover it. Nor the man-fear staring at him out of her eyes.

You'd kind of think the thought of her having that body . . . Well, it wasn't anything that should of made a man hate her—but it made Cardigan hate her. It had filled his head with an unreasoning anger and it still could do it every time he thought of her. While he'd been riding and sweating and risking everything he ever had hoped for in the choking dust and heat of this hellhole luckier guys had got them women like that—double-breasted doo-dads with creamy smooth bodies, that washed themselves and smelled sweet and purty.

Every time he thought of it it made him curse. He'd been ripe for trouble—for almost any fool thing, when that daffy Jupe Krailor had shown him the paper with the Heart and Hand column he had got off the Tombstone stage.

Cardigan hadn't hardly dared believe his own eyes. All them women wanting to come out here? Why the hell would a stall-fed Eastern filly—with every last thing you'd expect 'em to howl for—want to come out into this godforsaken country? It didn't make sense—but they did. There'd been three of 'em in that column alone fairly frothin at the mouth to get themselves out here! Seemed like all they wanted was a man to take care of them. Some of them even offered to send on their tintypes and two of them had claimed to have "character references"—like as if he cared about their goddam characters!

He'd come near to tearing that damned paper up, he'd been that disgusted to come on it so late. A St. Louis paper nearly six weeks old! Any fool could have told you any woman in her senses wouldn't of passed up her chances for six whole weeks—not without, by grab, there was something ailin her!

But the thought of those women wouldn't let him alone. Three of 'em eating their hearts out to get here and him, Kurt Cardigan, feeling so horny he was just about ready to climb on a squaw!

He'd waited till the rest had rolled up for the night, till he couldn't hear another dang thing but their snoring; then he'd crept from his blankets and hunted that paper. Had found it, too, and had tucked it away where he'd have it handy to study it over when he got off alone.

He could still remember how his hands had shook smoothing out that paper when he'd found the right page again. It was just like he'd been in a shakin fever and he'd thought he'd never hold it still enough to read it. One of them women didn't want to leave town. Three or four wanted local sports, gents with property, fellers with a business. A couple of more which had wanted to come West didn't sound like nothing he would want no truck with.

But the other one— Damn! He could still quote her words, every dadburned one of them:

REFINED YOUNG LADY, vivacious, 23, despising cold toast, coo-coo clocks and close relatives, desires correspondence with brown-eyed rancher, preferably one living west of the Pecos. Object, matrimony. Address: Miss Docie Balinett, 5486 Rimboldt Street, St. Louis, Mo.

Docie.
Docie Balinett! Just like docie-do in a brush-popper's hoedown. Docie. . . . By God, it even *sounded* like class!

He had given himself all the arguments but he'd known all the time he was going to write—and why not? Sure, some guy had likely landed her already, but it didn't cost no fortune for a man to find out and what gent ever really and truly hit his stride till he got hitched up to a female woman? Hell's hinges! This here was a damn tough country and it took a pretty salty feller to lick it. There'd been times he'd been so hungry his belly had thought his throat had been cut, but he'd have the laugh on these bastards yet. He'd come into this country to make his mark and, by God, he'd sure as hell make it!

That was the Irish in him; the Cardigan heritage, the red blood of his forebears than ran hotly through him, as ready to welcome a fight as a frolic. Pride—that was it! Well, he knew what pride was. Pride was something his kind had to have. Deep inside him a man might not care for all the things he did—might be downright sorry for some of them; but he'd keep it inside him. There was no good looking back and no good in excuses; excuses was for guys that couldn't tough a thing out. Well, they'd get no excuses from Cardigan. When he shoved his chips out they were out there to stay.

And there was no damn pride in drifting. You had to make a stand someplace. It was all in finding out what you could do, where your natural bent lay and in sinking your roots down. That was another good reason for having a woman; it gave a man something to tie to.

Well, he'd tried about everything the West had to offer from chasing cows' tails to mule skinning. He had driven a stage. He had been a freighter. He'd gone down in the ground like a goddam worm but what had it got him? He'd thought to cut the mustard that time he'd tried ranching . . . on the level, that is; but you could have it, and the drought and the maverickers and the whoopin redskins—you could have the whole push, and welcome.

There was easier ways than playing nursemaid to a bunch of dumb horn-clacking crazy damn cattle. You might as well prospect to be a real sucker. Work your damn tail off for some rich banker. No banker owned *him*—not Kurt Cardigan, damn their eyes! When Cardigan opened his mouth men listened. They didn't give him no back talk. Kurt Cardigan had things; he had a damn nice spread tucked away in the mountains and cattle and horses in uncounted numbers. And he had, moreover, a way with a pistol that men considered before they opened their jaws to do any yappin.

He slapped the big pistol that swung at his hip and twisted his head and threw a wink at the agent: "I'm goin' to drift over yonder an' feed my face. If that stage gets in . . . if somebody comes here askin' for me just remember you never heard tell of me——savvy?"

That was how he figured to take care of Docie.

Without she was a heap bigger fool than he thought, she damn sure wouldn't be expecting no different. She was probably all right. She hadn't made no offer to pass on her tintype which he figured she would if she had been at all worried.

She'd be a looker all right. He didn't doubt that. Five foot seven she had said in her letter. That would be about right—make her have to look up to him. It gave her plenty of frame to hang her meat on; he reckoned she'd be built like a tin-roofed smokehouse. That's what he wanted, a good rugged woman. A man couldn't spend all his time in a bed. By God, in this country you had to be practical.

He guessed she could handle the yard chores all right. Once he'd shown her how she could probably string fence. He kind of smiled a little thinking what a help she'd be around there. He'd let her spade up that patch northeast of the house. . . . She'd probably want to put in a truck garden for them; a woman, he reckoned, might get tired of boiled beans. He could damn well do with a little change himself.

Yep! A woman had her place, no getting around it; a man didn't rightly do no living till he had himself a woman around. He expected she could cook like nobody's business and just the thought of that bare white skin she'd have under her bustle was enough to get a guy hot all over.

He sucked in his breath with an impatient curse and glared out over the sunbaked miles like he'd fetch that stage by sheer force of willpower. If she stacked up right and took to the country he would tog her out like a million dollars. He'd get her a rig with big red wheels and drive her down the main drag of Tucson and give all them bastards something to goggle at. "By cripes," they'd say, "there goes Kurt Cardigan! I kin remember that bird when he didn't hev a pot——an' lookit the lucky bastard now!"

By God he'd make their eyes bug out.

Maybe he had ought to get slicked up a little. Maybe he ought to buy him a new shirt or something. He threw a considering look at the Mercantile and laughed a little and kept on up the street toward the hash house. Time enough for that when he'd filled his belly. Hell, maybe she wouldn't be on this stage, maybe she wouldn't get in till tomorrow. Time enough to doll up after he'd looked her over.

It wasn't that he really doubted she'd suit him. But this

country had long since taught him it was smarter to play your cards clost to your chest than to wish you had later when you didn't have no choice. He had done his part, he had sent her the money to get herself out here. If she didn't fill the bill she had nothing on him. She wouldn't know Cardigan from Adam's off ox.

This was what had finally decided him to write her. It didn't cost such a pile to get her out here and if she measured up he'd have something well worth it. And if she didn't measure up he could damn well saddle up his horse and hit out of here. He hadn't promised her nothing. He'd said straight out he'd have to look at her first, that he wasn't buying nothing—hogs or women—unseen.

But he'd told her he would pay the price of getting her out here—it was worth that much to get an armful of woman. Women was goddam scarce in this desert.

He went into the hash house and ordered his meal. He slanched a cursory glance at the other two eaters and promptly dismissed them as of no consequence. The farthest was a Mexican teamster slumped over his chile at the counter's other end. The other was a skinny dried-up old wart you didn't have to see but once to know was a desert rat.

A drummer came in with a fat cigar and flopped himself down on the stool next to Cardigan. He got out a white handkerchief and mopped his face. "Don't it ever cool off in this goddam country?"

The stove-up range cook that ran the place came up with Cardigan's grub and said sourly, "Them as don't like it ain't obliged t' stick around."

The drummer grunted. Then he gave him his order and mopped his face again. As he was putting the handkerchief back in his pocket he looked over at Cardigan and abruptly said heartily, "How they goin', pal? Been a long time since I seen you last. . . ."

Cardigan eyed him and reached for the butter. "Reckon you got me mixed up with somebody else."

"Oh, no—not me," the drummer said, grinning. "I never

forget a face. You're a horse trader, pal. Lemme see . . . it was over around—"

"You never seen me before in your life," Cardigan said, and the drummer stopped chewing and stared at him, startled. He stared like that for five or six seconds and then he took off his hat and peered inside it and ran pudgy fingers around the moist band. He looked at Cardigan again and then hastily away and covered his balding head with the derby and scratched three matches trying to kindle a cigar that was already lighted.

Cardigan ignored him and put away his plateful with a noisy relish. He got a second cup of coffee and another slab of pie.

The drummer didn't look to have much appetite. He got up pretty soon and took himself off. The prospector finished and shambled out also and the Mexican presently wiped a sleeve across his mouth and went over to the door where he dug out the makings and rolled himself a smoke.

Another man came in. He had a star on his shirtfront. He looked disinterestedly at Cardigan and took the stool recently warmed by the drummer. The cook came up wiping his hands on his apron.

"What'll it be this noon, Frank?"

By the cook's few words, and by that star he was sporting, Cardigan knew this man for the town's new marshal, Frank Esparza. He had never before met Esparza face to face and he eyed him covertly, thinking about him. He was a tired looking gent with a wrinkled face who told the cook he'd take the same as usual. This man had the rep, Kurt knew, of being honest and he had a known reluctance toward resorting to gunplay which had brought him the support of the town's big moguls who were against gunplay on general principles. Studying him now Cardigan dismissed most of the rumors he had heard. This fellow wasn't the kind to be afraid, or bluffed either.

Cardigan paid for his meal and got up and went out.

In the shade of the building the Mex teamster sat snoring. Cardigan stepped into the smash of the sun and scowlingly observed the stage hadn't come in yet. Then his glance, traveling farther, went still, bright and narrow.

A man by the hitchrack was eyeing his horse.

The cigar-smoking drummer. The dude in the derby.

2

COMPLICATIONS

WHEN HE saw that dude looking over his horse Cardigan knew straight off he had made a mistake. His fine run of luck had gone and rung in a joker and it made no difference that he didn't want trouble. Trouble was out there piling up fast, curling up with the heat off that limonite dust. It was in the sly eyes of that meddlesome drummer squinting this way and that as he sized up the points of Cardigan's dun.

That drummer was a kid with a match around powder.

If that feller had known him he'd of had better sense. But the guy was a dude, a damned puking tenderfoot who hadn't no knowledge of the customs of the country. A man who had known him would have thought a long while before poking his nose into Cardigan's business.

Cardigan knew he had better do something before that damned marshal put his face out the door. With that dude anything would be likely to happen. It was a cinch the guy's jaw would start swinging in a minute. He wouldn't have to say much. . . .

If it had been any horse but old Snuffy, Cardigan reckoned he'd been tempted to walk off and leave him. Not that that would solve anything in the long run but it might stave trouble off a little bit longer, long enough anyway to let him get clear of town.

Cardigan scowled, shook his head. This was one of those things you couldn't walk off from. There'd be plenty to remember he had ridden that horse.

Damn the dude anyway!

Two men were talking on the porch of a saloon that was twenty-five feet from the drummer's placement. A third gent was standing in the stage office doorway where a short time before the whole street had been empty; and worse—a lot worse—Frank Esparza was sitting dead in line with a window.

At the first sign of trouble he would jump for the door. That was what he got paid for.

"Damn!" Cardigan growled. He'd have to play this thing careful.

There was just one chance and, abruptly, he took it. He moved forward through the dust, feeling the burn of it through his bootsoles and feeling the burn of his anger, too.

He stopped by the man who stood eyeing the dun.

The drummer heard him. You could tell by the jump and swell of his shoulders, by the way he half turned with his guts all up where his swallower should have been.

"You're a-leavin' all right, but not on that horse, pard."

The words were pitched low but there was a throttled fierceness in Cardigan's voice that blanched the red look off the man's sunburned features. He opened his mouth but no sound came out. Cardigan saw the scared eyes jerk a look at his pistol and he laughed, short and harsh.

"Some guys," he drawled. "don't know when they're well off. Start siftin' along towards that stable, mister."

The drummer's face glistened. "You got me wrong—"

"I got you all right. You got that part straight."

The drummer's parched tongue scraped across his dry lips. Then he stiffened, went still, glaring back at Cardigan, outrage tautening the coat about his shoulders.

"You look kinda young to cash in," murmured Cardigan.

A hot wind flew off the roadway, bringing its smell of scorched dust and fluttering the scarf ends at Cardigan's throat.

"You—you wouldn't dare. . . ." the man muttered, and again that short laugh came out of Cardigan.

"Git movin', mister."

The sound of the hash house's screen door banging made a sharp report in the street's hot quiet and Cardigan said with a plainer impatience: "Git goin'—git goin'," and started forward.

The drummer fell back. He flung a trapped look out over the roadway but Cardigan's own look never wavered. It stayed hard on the drummer and he put out a hand and touched him lightly; and the man whirled away from that touch with a snarl.

Their steps sounded loud on the rough board planking and Cardigan's neck felt cold where the whipped—up wind flung grit across it. But he did not look around.

They came to the stableyard. The man, with a half-defiant glance, turned around.

"Right on into the stable," directed Cardigan, and a sullen growl came out of the drummer. "Stableman's a friend of mine," Cardigan said. "If I was you I'd keep my trap shut."

The drummer kept going but there was nothing reassuring in the set of his shoulders.

Cardigan's lips tightened. Deep in the marrow of his bones he didn't like this. If ever a damn fool was perched on a powder keg that guy was Cardigan and Cardigan knew it.

There was just a bare chance his lie about the stableman would keep the dude's mouth shut. Cardigan had no friends and was well aware of it. Friendship was built on respect and affection and the working arrangements he'd flung up in this country had little in common with such sterling virtues.

Which was plenty all right so long as things ran smooth. But he had a black hunch all the smoothness was over, that the smoothness had ended when this bird in the derby had planked down his fanny on that stool in Jelks' hash house.

Who'd have thought a damn dude with a couple dumb questions could be threatening to wreck in a handful of moments what had taken long years of mighty close figuring to bring to the point where . . .

A red fog of anger surged over Kurt Cardigan when he heard voices sound rumbling out from behind where a pile of stacked barrels cut off all view of the stalls in the rear.

It was cool in here after the glare outside but Cardigan never noticed. A wicked impulse leaped through him and sent a hand to his gun butt and he stood that way, rocked and quivering and glaring, while he fought to put down the wild roar of his blood.

Gunplay wouldn't buy him nothing but trouble. Killing this dude would take a heap of explaining and there was a damn good chance his tongue wouldn't be up to it.

With a bitter reluctance he took his hand from the pistol. Anger still rowelled him. He took the dude by the throat. "Listen," he grated. "I've took off you about all that I aim to. Just keep that damn mouth shut. You're gettin' out of this country—just be thankful an' *git* out 'cause there's other ways of goin' than on the back of a horse!"

He didn't half know his own strength it looked like. Alls he'd done had been to shake the guy a little, yet when he let him go the dude's knees wabbled and he staggered in a circle like a chicken with its head off, finally bringing up gasping against a stack of sacked feed.

Cardigan gave him about ten seconds then he hauled him up and scooped up the derby and clapped it on his head. "If you open your face it will be the last time."

He gave the guy a shove toward the squabble of voices.

The livery keeper and another old codger were insulting each other over a game of seven up.

"Ed," Cardigan said, "this gent wants a horse. He's in a hell of a hurry. Had bad news—he's got to get outa here. Mebbe you better let him have that dun."

The stableman laid his cards down carefully. He looked at the dude and rasped his jaw. "Where's he got t' go?"

Cardigan scowled. "El Paso," he said. "Can you shake it up a little?"

"We-ell, I tell you, Kurt. I ain't got that dun. I sold—"

"You got that apron-faced roan?"

"Yeah, I got that roan but he's lamed up a little—"

"What about that buttermilk filly?"

"He could hev her, I guess. But she'll come a little high. You recollect I—"

Sweat crept out across Cardigan's cheekbones. "How much?" he said blackly.

"Well, that filly ort t' bring about eighty-five dollars."

"He'll pay it. You'll have to throw in some gear."

"That'll be extry—another twenty-five dollars. I can't rightly spare—"

"Where's she at?"

"I'll fetch her." The stableman picked up a rope. "I got her outside . . . she might be jest a little bit high—Kin this feller ride?"

The possibility that he couldn't hadn't occurred to Cardigan. He scowled and said, "Sure. Shake it up. Which saddle?"

"Expect he'll hev to take that McClellan."

Cardigan got it and picked up a bridle, motioned the drummer ahead of him. The man's look turned ugly. So did Cardigan's. The dude got to moving.

They watched the old man put his rope on the filly. With her taffy-colored hide and white mane and tail she looked so set up Cardigan came near to wishing he hadn't never sold her. Another thought came and he knew he'd been right. These flashy-colored hides were too easy to remember.

He sleeved the sweat off his cheeks and gave the old man the saddle, adjusting the bridle while the stableman cinched up.

"That'll be a hundred an' ten," the stableman said and Cardigan looked at the drummer.

The dude put a hand inside his coat and the bones shaping Cardigan's face showed plainer; but the dude brought his hand out carefully, empty.

"Must've left my wallet at the hotel," he mumbled, and Cardigan nodded.

He pulled out a roll and peeled off the money.

"The hoss-breedin' business must be doin' all right," grinned the stableman jocularly, winking at the drummer. But the dude didn't smile. The old man sighed. "Some of yore folks sick or somethin'?"

The dude looked at Cardigan and didn't say anything.

"Well, you wanta watch out," the stableman said. "Keep

yore eyes wide open goin' through that pass. Them redskins is riled. Ain't a one been in town here for more'n two weeks—they been brewin' up somethin', you kin bet on that."

Some thought palely twisted the drummer's features.

Cardigan snorted.

He bent over the makings and shaped up a smoke. When he tongued the paper his teeth threw a shine against the tan of bronzed features. "He'll git by all right—I'll see to that."

He cursed under his breath when the stableman's eyes touched him, curious, considering. "Goin' through with him, eh?"

The drummer looked like he would lose his dinner.

The stableman said in a tone tinged with envy, "Sure wisht *I* could sell some stuff to the Cavalry. I'd make 'em come after 'em—you wouldn't ketch me pushin' no stock through that pass. Not with the way them Injuns been actin'."

Cardigan said, "I ain't pushin' no stock. I'm goin' to hunt for that stage."

"What good'll that do? Ain't nothin' but redskins—"

"My God!" the dude cried. "Are you kiddin'?"

The stableman looked at him. "A man don't kid about Injuns, son."

Conflicting emotions were tugging at Cardigan. The whereabouts of that woman, the need he felt of finding her were companion worries that, combined with inclination, were pulling him one way while the even greater need concerned with this dude was ever more strongly urging him another. He knew he ought to get out and hunt that stage—he'd money tied up in that goddam woman and he sure didn't want no redskins scalping her. But he'd money tied up in other things, too, and this puking dude could lose it for him if he got to swinging his jaw around. And the guy held the cards to make him lose more than money.

Once loose on a horse there was no telling what he'd do. He might run to the marshal. He might hit for Camp Grant. . . .

If only, thought Cardigan, *I'd kept my damn mouth shut!*

That was where he'd slipped, back there in Jelks' hash house. Instead of laughing it off he'd played tough with the feller. The guy would not be forgetting Kurt Cardigan now. He would not be forgetting that dun horse either.

He'd be swinging his jaw the first chance he got.

There was one thing Cardigan would sure have to do. He would have to stick with him. He'd have to stick with him anyways till he got beyond where his damn talking would matter. And that meant for sure at least to Dragoon Springs.

Under his breath Kurt Cardigan cursed.

There had ought to be a law against dudes, goddam it!

And the worst of it was he had to pick up that horse, that dun he had hitched to the stage office tierack.

He thought too much of that dun to leave him— Why, old Snuffy and him was pardners almost! He'd as soon cut off his right arm as leave Snuffy.

Yet he knew that was what a smart man would do.

He sleeved the sweat off his face again and scowled. A man was a fool to let feeling for a horse ever get in the way of good sense that way. He always had been a fool about Snuffy. . . .

He sure hated to haul that dude back uptown. But he couldn't afford to leave the guy here—he'd run off at the mouth till hell wouldn't have it. Like to run off uptown if he saw that marshal—the guy was scared enough to. That Injun talk had turned him plumb green.

Cardigan's scowl grew blacker.

There was no use blinking it. He couldn't leave the horse. All feelin aside, that dun had the best set of heels in the country. Speed might count before he got done with this.

He had sure got himself into one fine mess! If he hadn't sent for that woman—but wishes wouldn't butter no parsnips. He had to get this crazy dude out of here and he sure couldn't leave him while he went after Snuffy. He'd just have to take the guy with him.

The time for thinking, he reckoned, was a considerable while past.

"George," he said, breaking into the stableman's rambling discourse, "we better git over an' fetch your wallet an' we better start humpin' or you won't never make it."

"I'll go fix you a bill o' sale—"

"You do that," Cardigan told him. "I'll drop by for it next time I'm through town." He looked at the dude. "Let's git goin'. You can lead that filly till we git to the hotel."

He took the dude by the arm and urged him streetward.

Soon as they got well away from the stable Kurt stopped. "I'll take that hundred an' ten now," he said, and the dude passed it over without any argument. He was too plain scared to even open his mouth.

Cardigan looked at him. The guy was scared plenty, no doubt about that. There didn't look to be any more fight in that feller than a man would expect to get from a field mouse.

Cardigan peered up the street. He didn't have many choices. He had to get the horse. He had to keep hold of this guy but it would be doubling the risk to tote him back up-town. And he sure couldn't 'e him, not unless he gagged him, and to leave him like that would just be asking for trouble.

He guessed he'd better chance his luck and leave the guy loose.

"George," he said, soft and careful, "I've got to go fetch my horse. You kin slope if you want to but you'd better wait here. There ain't nothin' in this world that's any quicker than a bullet."

3

GUN TOWN MARSHAL

*C*ARDIGAN, whistling a bawdy tune, struck off up the street at a saddle-cramped swagger. You would never have guessed by his cocky look that inside his pants his knees were shaking, or that his heart was banging around in his gullet like a shut-in bird trying to fly through a window. He would not have been one bit surprised to have heard the departing clatter of that filly. If the guy had any sense at all he would know damn well no feller would be fool enough to shoot him in a town. If he had any sense he'd jump onto that mare and take off through the greasewood like a bat out of Carlsbad.

But if the dude was doing it he was being mighty quiet. Cardigan could catch not the faintest sound of hoofbeats. He heard the drone of a fly, a restless horse stamping, but no commotion of any sort broke the drowsy hush of the noontime quiet. He could only hope the damn lunkhead would stay there.

With that blasted stage better than three hours late and him eating his heart out about that woman you would think he had enough on his mind!

He tried to figure where that dude could have seen him. "You're a horse trader, pal," the damn fool had chortled.

There was only one way he could have gotten that notion; the dude must have seen him with a bunch of horses.

And it must have been around a town. And Kurt hadn't been near a town in six months or he never would have got so het up for a woman.

That thought pulled his mind back around to Docie and the goddam stage that was three hours late. Them redskins *had* been acting queer lately. Used to be you could see a bunch any time squatting with their prats hunkered down by a porch edge and no more look on their fat lumpy faces than a guy could twist from the flat of a skillet. But this morning there hadn't been one stinking Injun. . . .

"Your name Cardigan?"

Cardigan stopped with his throat dry as cotton. He was almost even with the saloon's warped porch and the men who'd been on it weren't there any more. Asleep on his feet the dun dozed thirty feet away and it might just as well have been a full thirty miles for it was Frank Esparza who'd stepped into the sunlight, Frank Esparza who now stood

watching Kurt across five yards of questioning silence. Frank
Esparza, the town's new marshal.

"I said is your name Cardigan?"

"That's right," Cardigan said.

"Understand you raise horses."

There was in Cardigan then a sudden urge to violence.
It was a thing built up of all the years he had been here,
of all the things he had done and all the things he had tried to
do; an urge compounded of the plain expectations those
things had engendered.

But none of this thinking touched the surface of his features.
By a tremendous effort he held himself still. *Was this it?* he
wondered. *Was this how it was to be?*

He met the marshal's stare and nodded.

"That's right," he said again.

A kind of stillness settled round them, a charged sort of
quiet that might, it seemed to Cardigan, erupt at any moment. It had never occurred to him before that this street
could be so wide or so completely without sound.

A small wind whipped up and ran through the fronds of
the scaly-barked pepper trees while Esparza continued without movement to watch him.

The marshal lifted a hand then and scratched at his chest
and the stretch of the faded cotton shirt showed how well
good living had padded his belly. His eyes ran the loops of
Cardigan's gun belt and considered the pistol that weighted
his holster. Then they swiveled away and went across to the
horse, to that dozing dun Kurt had come here to fetch.

"Is that a horse of your raising?"

Cardigan stood very still and very softly sighed. He settled
his weight and tipped his head a little forward and he watched
the marshal's eyes and said: "Sure."

The man should have gone for his gun. It was the natural
thing for a marshal to do when a gent laid claim to a stolen
horse. It was the thing Kurt Cardigan had looked for, the
obvious answer to the cards turned up. When, instead, the

marshal merely smiled it threw Kurt Cardigan completely off balance. All his forces had been marshaled to meet and beat gunplay; he could not adjust himself that swiftly to such a sudden shift.

It left him weak in the knees and a sudden wild anger began churning his bowels, leaving the length of him drenched in cold sweat.

He looked at the man through a glaze of bright fury, at his white grinning teeth and the pink flabby jowls that hung down like old wattles. His hands itched to feel themselves around that fat throat.

The old fool was talking and the fostered care of six years in this country was a habit even stronger than Cardigan's anger. He forced himself to listen. "What was that again?"

"Understand you raise stock for the Cavalry."

For the Cavalry . . . Christ!

"I've sold 'em a few," Cardigan finally growled gruffly.

He was still mad and scared and he still didn't get it. This old gander talked like he held all the cards but he sure as hell wasn't playing it that way. If he knew so damned much why keep beating the bushes?

The marshal scratched himself again. "Is that stallion for sale?"

"Old Snuffy? Hell, no!"

Esparza nodded. "That's a mighty fine horse, Mister Cardigan. If he's a sample of the kind you're raisin' out there I expect I can throw some business your way. Tell you what— I'll ride out there . . ."

"Not right now—not with me you won't. I've got to git out an' hunt that stage."

"Hunt the stage?" The marshal's eyes showed surprise. "What would *you* be figurin' to hunt that stage for?"

"Well, by God! Ain't it late? Don't you know—"

"I can't see that it's any of your concern."

"It's about time *someone* was gittin' concerned!"

Cardigan brushed the marshal aside and went by him, un-looped the dun's reins and climbed into the saddle. With the muscles of his back all scringed up and cringing he wheeled the horse round and, without another look at the roan-cheeked lawman, put him down the road at a businesslike canter.

4

"THAT GODDAM STINKIN' DUDE!"

THERE ARE times when a man doesn't feel like thinking, when thoughts and the things conjured by them are matters best left entirely alone. This was one of those times but the knowledge did not tend to cool Cardigan or lessen the savage turmoil inside him. Had his thoughts been broncs he could have penned them up, but who could put his rope on worry?

It sure burned him up to think of the way that old coot had talked to him, leading him on like a snake-hipped hooker and never even putting a hand near his smokepole.

Just the same, in a way, he was glad Esparza hadn't. Shooting was the last thing he wanted right now. Right now all he wanted was to find that woman and he couldn't do that till he got rid of this dude.

To hell with Esparza! Let him run his bluffs if it made him feel good. It he had known anything he would of played it different, he never would have let Cardigan get away from him. And that was for sure!

He gave a sudden reckless laugh. It wasn't likely the marshal was even suspicious. And what if he was? Let him go to the ranch and look around for himself. A fat lot of good that would do him. He could look till hell froze for all of Kurt Cardigan. There was no fancy art work on Cardigan's acres.

It was the horse right under him now that was dangerous. This red-maned buckskin with the flashing heels, this whirlwind, this hellcat, this crazy-headed outlaw that, despite every urge of common sense and good judgment, Kurt Cardigan could never quite bring himself to kill.

Oh, he'd meant to, all right; he had sure aimed to do it. When the boys fetched him in with the fat mares that night he had cursed them out proper. "Why you goddam fools," he'd said—"*look* at him! A give-away horse if I ever seen one!" Danger was bred in his very bones—in those cat-quick feet and rolling eyes, in the taffy-colored hide and that lean jagged blaze on his face like white lightning. "A picture horse!" Kurt had lashed at them, furious. "God damn it to hell! What you apes tryin' to do—get my neck stretched for me?"

He'd been plumb against the red dun till he'd learned every man of them shared his feelings. They had grabbed him by mistake, caught him up with a band of foaling mares. A range stallion. A wild, untamed devil who never had known the feel of a saddle, they had fetched him along to see which could break him. They had fetched him down from Wyoming some place. "Hell, there ain't no Wyomin' waddies round here," Curly Lahr had scoffed. "What the Christ are you scairt of?"

Knowing better, knowing well what a threat that yellow stud represented, he had let the horse stay. If the boys wanted to ride him let them have their fun. If they didn't plumb kill him he could shoot the horse later.

That was the way he had looked at it then.

So they'd all tried their hands. They were a tough lot, too, but that damned dun was tougher. He was the orneriest horse they had ever encountered—a biting, kicking, sunfishing fool. He had killed one bungler. He had crippled another.

The crippled guy, Hennessy, like to lost his damn mind. "Rope me that sonuvabitch! Tie up the bastard!" he had sobbed through the bloody froth on his lips. "I'll fix that devil—ear 'im down!" he'd raged. And he'd have done it, too, if Kurt had stayed out of it. With his broken leg dragging he had crawled through the dust with a knife in his hand. Oblivious to the pain of his hoof-caved ribs he'd have cut the horse to ribbons in his fury if Cardigan had not stopped him.

Kurt had never been able to figure out why he'd bothered to step in and save that horse. It was against all reason. He had rightly recognized the horse as a menace but he hadn't let them kill him and he wouldn't let them geld him. As a matter of fact, after that first day he wouldn't let the men touch him.

They hadn't liked it a little bit. They'd eyed him like he'd taken leave of his senses. "You'd better kill that bayo coyote," Lahr said, "before he puts another notch in his tail."

That was mighty sound reasoning, best advice in the world and Cardigan knew it, yet he'd made no effort to get rid of the horse. And he wasn't a man to be swayed by sentiment, cynically rejecting all sentiment as weakness—which it was.

He regarded the horse as a constant hazard yet continued to work with him, knowing a tremendous elation at each small sign of progress. That dun was smarter than a heap of humans, but a wild streak in him made him savagely distrustful of anything smelling like a man-critter to him. Yet he came to whinny at Cardigan's approach and in the end suffered Cardigan to ride him.

It was the proudest day in Cardigan's life.

The men did not share his enthusiasm. They profanely predicted he would rue the day he had knocked the knife out of Hennessy's hand. "Sure you're ridin' him, but that don't prove a goddam thing! That bastard'll kick you hell west an' crooked!"

Cardigan laughed at them.

Lahr had pinned the name of Jubal Jo on the horse but most of the time Cardigan called him Snuffy—which he sure as hell had been till Cardigan tamed him.

With Kurt the big stallion was wonderfully gentle. You'd have thought Kurt had brought him up on a bottle if you hadn't known how he had come to get hold of him. But the men shook their heads. "That goddam hoss'll kill him yet!"

They'd become inseparable. For a man who considered sentiment a weakness that horse took up an awful lot of Kurt's time. For weeks at a stretch he would seldom be seen on any other horse. "This goddam dun can do anything," he told them. When Lahr heard about it he twisted his face up and spat, disgusted. "It's a wonder he don't take the damn bronc t' bed with 'im!"

Cardigan wasn't by nature an introspective man, being mostly given over to taking things as he found them, but there were times when he wondered himself about that horse, about the feeling that seemed to have sprung up between them. It was a damned funny thing when you stopped to consider it.

He knew well enough the risk he was taking, pirootin around on a stolen horse. In this kind of country where a horse was a man's only means of transportation—where, indeed, his very life might depend on whether he had a horse available—the end of a gent accused of horse-thievery was apt to be sudden and frequently uncomfortable.

He had never, he thought, tried to fool himself. The danger in having this horse around lay not in the animal's own proclivities but in the chance of his being recognized. It made no difference that Kurt himself hadn't stolen him. Snuffy did not belong to him—that was the wedge any lawman would work on. Cardigan had no intention of returning him and had announced this decision when he'd answered "Sure" to the marshal's question.

Wyoming was a long ways off. Who around here could dispute his right to this blaze-faced dun once he'd gotten that drummer out of the country?

Remembrance of the dude put an end to his thinking and he leaned forward in the saddle, abruptly going still, staring.

With a smothered oath he pulled the horse to a stop.

The dude was gone.

He wasn't even in sight!

With a curse Cardigan kneed the dun forward. The blabber-mouthed bastard was probably back in the stable spilling his guts to that nosey liveryman!

But one glance up the lane that led to the stable disclosed no sign of the buttermilk filly.

He looked at the hoof-tracked dust where he'd left them

and there, sure enough, was the crazy nump's shoe prints. There was where he had climbed up onto the horse. And there was the filly's sign, off at a walk, curling round behind the buildings, making for that pile of old crates behind the Mercantile. Yes . . . and there, by God, was where he'd poured on the leather—straight out into the goddam desert!

The crazy tenderfoot fool!

How long did he think he would last out in that stuff? He would get himself lost before he sweated a blister—was probably lost right now. He'd go tearing around in a thirst-frantic circle and play out his horse within ten minutes of town. It was the way of his kind, it was what they all did when they got off alone into the quiet of the wastelands. Never used no sense, just kept running in circles like a bunch of fool chickens with their heads cut off. The buzzards would be picking his bones by tomorrow.

Unless Kurt went after him.

He sat there a moment and thought about that.

Why the hell should he?

Hadn't the dadburned peckerneck been enough trouble? The guy had asked for this! He wasn't nothing to Kurt but a threat and a menace.

The smart thing to do was to ride off and forget him. Without that dude, Frank Esparza could whistle. There wasn't one chance in ten the guy would ever make it back.

Cardigan squinched up his eyes and looked off into the glare. A hot wind was blowing off those sun-blasted ridges, a wind that would fry a man's skin like a stove top. Nothing could live out there that didn't know it—nothing but the hoot owls, the gophers and the goddam snakes. In the blinding glare of that brassy heat that damfool drummer couldn't last two hours.

And besides, by God, he'd got to hunt for that woman!

Christ! To think of her alone on that stage—and on account of Kurt Cardigan! You couldn't get around it. He had sent her the money to get herself out here. And she'd said she would come; said he didn't have to take her if she didn't suit his fancy. By God it took real guts to do a thing like that to come half across the country on the chance of a guy you hadn't never seen liking you!

What happened to that dude wasn't no skin off *his* nose. If that dude had got his rights he'd be damn dead anyway for stickin his mug into someone else's business. Most of these birds would of bashed his damn head in.

Cardigan knuckled the sweat from his eyes and scowled blackly.

Mostly Butterfield's stages ran right on the dot. His drivers didn't lallygag around picking daisies. A busted axle or a wheel off couldn't account for them being this late. They were used to such things and could make shift in spite of them. That stage was bogged deep down in trouble and it was dollars to doughnuts the trouble wore feathers.

With a growl he fed old Snuffy the steel, whirled him suddenly round and pulled him up with an oath. "That goddam stinkin' dude!" he cursed, and bitterly took up the drummer's trail.

5

STAGE FROM EL PASO

*T*HE HEAT boiled down like the wrath of God. You could see its filmy shimmer curling off the rocks, you could feel it in your nostrils like a searing flame. In all that waste nothing moved in Kurt's vision save the blue-gray peaks that smoked in the sun dance.

He had thought to find the dude fairly quick, had been sure of it, but already he'd ridden for one solid hour and the damned fool's tracks still unreeled before him. It was against all the logic of Cardigan's experience that a man as unused to the desert as that dude looked would have stayed on his horse and kept going this long.

One thing surprised him even more than that. The guy hadn't chased himself round in circles. He hadn't foundered the filly in a panic for haste. The tracks led straight south-east as an arrow, as straight toward St. David as though he were heading there. Yet how could he be? The guy was an outlander knowing nothing of this country, knowing nothing but he need to get away from Kurt Cardigan.

Cardigan sleeved his face and cursed.

He still hadn't figured what to do with the guy. He sure couldn't waste much more time on him, not nearly enough now to see him to the Springs—not, anyways, if he would find that woman. What a man ought to do was to put a bullet through him. That's what you'd do with a snake that attacked you—that's what you'd damn quick do with a Injun! Why should a man treat a dude any different? Only a dimwit would turn a snake loose to come back and maybe do a good job next time.

That was sound thinking. It was mighty good thinking Cardigan told himself, but he knew all-fired well it wasn't in him to do it. He was tough all right, but not that tough. There was a soft streak in him that was more damn dangerous to his health than that stallion. He could knock down a man in a fight and forget it. But he never had been able to bring himself to up and shoot another feller down in cold blood.

If the stinker would just cooperate a little . . . maybe fall off his horse and bash his damn head in, or kick off from the heat or get snake-bit or something. You sure wouldn't catch him crying about it.

But until that happened he felt bound to hunt him, even though he might begrudge every minute of the time.

He would a whole heap liefer be out hunting Docie. He *ought* to be hunting her, he told himself scowling. Just the thought of her out there alone, by God, was enough to make a guy throw up his breakfast.

The sun commenced slanting toward the Tucson Mountains and for the hundredth time Kurt stood up in his stirrups and sent a black glance over the desolate surroundings before sinking back with a frustrated curse. Nothing but cactus, desert growth and dust. Nowhere did anything move but the greasewoods. Nothing but heat and the white glare of emptiness curling away into lost horizons.

He knuckled the sweat from his burning eyes and pressed on again with his gaze on the tracks in the dry parched dust, convinced when he topped each yonder rise he would finally come up with the fleeing drummer. It was sheer damned hope for there was no truth in it.

It just didn't make sense that that yellow-shoed dude could keep ahead of him this way. It was surprising enough the guy stayed in the saddle. It strained belief that he should keep going this way mile after mile, maintaining his lead, without killing the filly.

But the filly was still going strong by the sign. Of course Cardigan wasn't really pushing his own horse—a man would be a fool to in this kind of heat; but that was just what you'd look for a damn dude to do. And the guy had been plenty scared to start with.

He wondered if the fellow had water, if the garrulous stableman had thought to provide him. He'd ought to have done it as a matter of course because Cardigan had said the dude was quitting the country, but he was damned if he could remember seeing any canteen.

That tenderfoot fool had ought to caved long ago. It just wasn't reasonable he should keep on going. Yet there were the filly's tracks.

There wasn't no chance the guy had fell off. Cardigan would have noticed; there would have been the changed gait of the filly besides. No horse without guidance would have gone this straight, nor this steady.

He threw a look at the sun. It was getting late. He looked again at the tracks. They'd been walking here, taking it easy just as if the guy was an old-timer at it. "Savin' his horse!" Cardigan told himself bitterly. He'd misjudged this guy plenty. By all the signs and signal smokes the guy wasn't going to cash in at all.

He scowled again at the sun that was barely an hour from the jagged crests of the western crags. He'd got to find him quick or yell calf rope. He sure couldn't trail no dude in the dark.

They mustn't be, he judged, much more than twenty miles from the town of St. David. It wasn't a town, really, but a settlement of Mormon farmers hubbed about a cross-trails store that among the country's cowhands was mainly known for its whisky. North by east of this place, about an easy day's ride, lay Camp Grant and the U. S. Cavalry.

Roughly calculating his position Cardigan figured he was not more than five or six miles to the south of the stage road; a couple miles farther east it would swing directly north to skin through the Pass and whipsaw its way through the Dragoon Mountains. They were getting right into the Apache country and if a man set any value on his hair he had damn well better be keeping his eyes peeled.

Still more than half convinced he must sight the dude soon, Cardigan pressed on. But at dark he had not caught him. The guy was still driving straight as a string for St. David. He might or he might not yap when he got there but one thing you sure had to hand to them Mormons—they were almighty good at minding their own business.

"T' hell with 'im!" Cardigan said, pulling up. The moon wouldn't rise for another three hours and he was damned if he was going to hang around here waiting on the extremely off chance he might still catch that dude. Any guy with the wit to get himself this far would sure have the sense to keep on going. It was a heap more important that he locate Docie, which was what he had wanted to do in the first place. He'd given them Injuns too much time already.

He cast about in his mind for the likeliest place where whatever had happened to the stage might have happened. There were too many choices. That Dragoon country was an ambusher's paradise, a mighty rough country, crossed and crisscrossed with ridges and arroyos, a land of mesquite and yucca where ambush was possible at every turn. The nearer he got to that slot of a Pass the rougher the country was going to become; but the chances were—if Apaches were responsible for the stage's non-appearance—he would find the stage, or what was left of it, someplace in the canyon. The stage road through this dusty hell was strewn with the wrecks of abandoned wagons sticking their gaunt ribs out of the sands among the bleached-white bones of mules and horses.

He was glad he hadn't touched his water, he'd probably need it all before he got done with this. One good thing about redskins—most of their devilment that was sprung in the dark was generally geared to those hours that were closest to dawn. This gave him a leeway of about six hours before he would have to start watching for them. He wished he could say as much for the whites who made this region their stamping ground, but he knew their kind for a chancy lot and there was no predicting their actions.

He pushed steadily on through the deepening night, conserving his horse but determined, if he could, to make the west end of the Pass by dawn.

He kept away from the stage road. Proximity to that would be a heap too likely to decrease a man's chances. There was a pile of riffraff in this country, men run out of more settled regions, and he'd troubles enough without inviting their attention. Several times he detoured to avoid darkened camps, warned off by the smell of woodsmoke, by the snores of stertorous sleepers or by the sounds of horses rattling their hobbles. And always, through the slow-passing night, he kept thinking of Docie till he couldn't hardly stand it.

He saw her in a thousand guises and none of them calculated to cheer a man up. While before he had pictured how she'd look in a bed, he saw her now through a film of horror. If those damned red bastards had taken her . . .

Such thoughts set him wild, left him filmed with sweat; but he wasn't a man to fool himself. He knew mighty well what her chances were, what likelihood there was of him finding her unharmed.

He got jumpier than ever as the hours drew closer to the crack of dawn. What if his horse stepped into a dog hole or slipped in the rocks and broke a leg? What if he couldn't locate the stage? Suppose he'd guessed wrong and overshot it?

He commenced hearing things that had no existence outside

of his head and once he'd have sworn he was followed. Dawn was less than half an hour away when he broke through a thicket of chaparral and came onto the rutted stage road.

The Pass lay just yonder. Through the damp gray gloom he could see the dark sides of the canyon and his hair started crawling as he caught the dark bulk of a twisted mass not hardly a hundred yards ahead. Something nauseous gripped the cold void of his belly as he rummaged the shadows about that thing and could find no movement, no life about it.

He sat stiffly unmoving for five long minutes while his bitter eyes raked the shadows round it, probing each bush, each rock and each hollow. He almost flung himself out of the saddle when a cactus wren flitted out of a nearby cholla. With a harsh curse, then, he started forward, and cursed again when he came to the thing at the edge of the road.

It was nothing but the wreck of an abandoned wagon.

Yet the scare stayed with him. He had been too long in this harsh land to pass up the value of sudden hunches. He had stayed too long on the trail of that dude and fear lay cold as froglegs in him.

He walked the dun into the canyon, rifle across his pommel, eyes narrowed, searching the rimrock with all the care in him. Fear and hate clenched his jaws till his back teeth ached and his muscles were tight as drawn bowstrings. He tried to shut thoughts of Docie out of his mind yet it almost seemed he could hear her screams and his back and belly were cold with sweat.

It was much lighter now, day was almost at hand, but no sound of twittering birds came to ease him. The canyon was choked with a breathless hush. Each fall of the stallion's hoofs seemed loud as a gunshot in that quiet. Cardigan knew what those devils could do to a woman they didn't want to keep for squaw's work.

The thought of it almost made him retch.

He watched how the sun suddenly brightened the east, flinging its thin clear light on the rimrocks, noticing how the advent of it seemed to deepen the canyon's solitude, making the shadowed sides more dark, more suggestive of ambush, of hidden eyes watching; and he pictured the stage toiling up the grade with the grunting horses digging into their collars, great muscles bulging, harness creaking with the awful strain as the iron-rimmed wheels ground against the shale and went noisily jolting over the outcrops—the sudden stop, the driver's oath, the shearing scream of a woman as the hideous painted faces ringed them and the ululating cries of the shrieking Apaches rose and lifted into a paean of hate.

He cursed himself for a daunsy fool and touched his heels to the dun's wet flanks, only to grunt and pull up sharply as they topped a rise of hard-baked ground and saw the abandoned stage before them half capsized in the dusty road.

It was appalling the way that Abbott-Downing looked with its elegance rent and slashed to ribbons, the splintered boards of its seats all over, its stout leather braces scarred with axe bites, its storm curtains hanging in dismal tatters.

The bloating shapes of two dead horses grotesquely lay amid the tangle of harness and a man was sprawled near the first on his face and it was plenty plain he would never get up.

Cardigan stared, too sick to curse. He wanted to retch but he couldn't do it. His stomach was tied in a rigid knot and he thought for a minute he would go clean crazy as he thought of the woman who had been on this stage.

A merciful numbness seized his mind holding back the grisly thoughts that clawed it and the reins groaned in the clutch of his hand as he kneed Jubal Jo toward that carnage.

Another man lay in the dust of the road with both hands grabbed to his blackened chest where the shaft of an arrow showed between them while the skin of his face hung down like gristle.

There were no more corpses.

Three times, very watchful, he rounded the stage but he had seen them all. Arrows pin-cushioned its sides and there were more arrows sticking from the two dead horses.

He sat the big dun looking down at them sickly, seeing where the others had been hacked from the harness and driven off when the marauders left. He saw the slashed mail sacks laying in the road and the litter of torn-up letters around them, fluttering now in the early breeze; the scattered bags and luggage with the knife scars on them. But always his eyes kept returning to the horses, to the boot tracks that showed around the tangle of harness.

He turned the dun finally and rode nearer to the stage, then around to the boot and to the sprung-open door on the stage's other side. And at each pause he nodded with his heart beating wilder.

Boot tracks everywhere, not a mark of a moccasin.

How long he sat there staring down at them he had no idea but his face, when at last he lifted it, had the look of something pounded from metal. His hands were cramped from their grip of the reins.

It was not Apaches he had to reckon with. This was the work of renegade whites.

6

MAN TRACKS

To A MAN as familiar with sign as Cardigan, it was no trick at all to pick up their trail. There'd been five in the party and they'd struck off north quick as ever they'd gotten outside the canyon, driving the stolen stage stock with them. One of them had the girl up in front of him, the marks of that horse showing deeper, more sharp lines; it was a pretty safe guess that guy was the leader.

It would be hard to say which bunch this was. There was a pile of tough outfits roving the country preying on prospectors and any small fry that looked worth the trouble. Men without code, these were, without scruple, wolves of the chaparral, savage and deadly.

This was their stamping ground, a land with blood spilled across every foot of it, a range sliced up into draws and gullies, split and quartered till at times you'd have thought there could be no crossing it; but always the outlaws found a way and, although sometimes they left no trail at all, Cardigan managed to hang and rattle.

It was not easy. It took a heap more time than he cared to give it and was a task at once calculated to wear a man down and try the most dogged tenacity, beset as it was every stride of the way by the ever-present threat of ambush.

These border ruffians were a wily breed, much practiced in the art of eluding pursuit and fully aware of the fate they courted. They overlooked no bets save the one he had constantly to guard against—ambush, and he was amazed they did not try that as well. They might try it yet. They probably never dreamed they would be followed so soon—all this ducking and dodging was a natural routine with their kind of gentry.

Not for a moment dared Kurt let down his vigilance. One moment could be an eternity sometimes. The time required for a finger to squeeze a trigger could be infinitesimal and one bullet could finish him, could stop him forever. Until his burning eyes went blind from the glare he was bound to keep them prowling the slopes, scanning each thicket, each shade patch and pocket. It was the price he must pay for continued living.

This was a canny breed, cunning as foxes to throw off the hunter. Doubling and twisting they antigodled continually, employing every guile in their feral natures that might tend to confuse any following party.

The ledges drove Cardigan to most of his cursing and the renegades seemed to be always finding them, great barren outcrops of rock long winnowed of soil by gale and cloudburst, rust-red, blue-green, sometimes black with mineral. Many of these he was forced to circle several times before he could pick up their sign again, and, such times, he acted like a man possessed.

Heat lay over these barrens like smoke and a scorched smell came off this bone-dry land that was like the stench of a burned-out kettle. Lifeless it stretched like a faded blanket, monotonous, immeasurable, to the desolate peaks that, like drunken sentries, tottered and danced on the brassy horizons.

The rock points of the Dragoon Mountains fell behind and

gradually turned blue in the shimmering heat and, by noon, the sign of the quarry had grown noticeably fresher. Patience, Kurt felt, was nearing its reward. He could no longer doubt he was overtaking them. Though his bloodshot eyes could not yet pick them up he was convinced they were not now far ahead of him. He wet his mouth with the lowering contents of his government-issue canteen and gave half a hatful of the tepid water to the horse that had fetched him all this way and again pressed forward.

Shortly after one, following the sign up out of a wash, he came onto a yucca-studded bench of sand and reined Jubal in with a bitter curse. Less than two hours ago this bench, by the sign, had been the scene of a running fight. The ground was crossed and recrossed with tracks in a way that left small doubt of what had happened. To Cardigan the evidence was completely convincing. Coming out of that wash the renegade crew had run head-on into a file of cavalrymen. Panic had routed the stage-robbing crew, sent them ducking and dodging, every man for himself. There had been no pause, no chance for palavering. They had whirled for the brush going hellity-larrup and it was useless, in that scuffed-up sand, to attempt to track down individual sign.

Cardigan had neither the time nor the patience. He put the dun into an immediate circle, scanning for sign of that heavy horse's hoofs. It was the only sign Kurt gave a damn about, the double-burdened horse that was carrying Docie.

He rode twenty yards in the start of his circle, changed his mind, reined the dun to the left to cut it larger, to commence where the trail was less tangled by churning. He had to go clear into the greasewood before he found tracks that were sufficiently separate to read without getting out of the saddle. Speed right now was all that counted. He was hunting for sign he could read at a run and he found it before a scraggly mesquite thicket.

A trail of broken branches led through it and, riding his stirrups, Kurt Cardigan followed. The trail came out on the farther side in a welter of converging tracks and there stopped, forever, beneath the still-warm body of the man's dead horse.

Cardigan felt as though fate had doublecrossed him. His hands got to shaking. All the strength fell out of him and his weight dropped into the saddle heavily. He sat there like a man gone blind.

"God damn it!" he said savagely, and stared at the dead black horse in a fury. But he was too used up to swear any more. He felt spent as a wrung-out dishrag.

He looked at that dead black horse without words and at the green-backed flies that droned off it angrily as he kneed the blowing dun in closer to have a try at the brand on its top-side shoulder, but the mark wasn't any iron he recognized.

"Hell!" he said then. "What difference does the goddam brand make!"

Then his mind commenced working, began sorting things out again. This was the horse and it was plenty dead. Where was the man—and where was Docie?

Being careful to avoid disturbing the tracks immediately around it, he skirted the horse and commenced a painstaking combing of the brush all around, but he wound up with no further sign of either. Baffled he came back to the black but the tracks there didn't tell him much. There were too many of them superimposed on each other. What Cardigan wanted was to find that man in the hope he might learn what had happened to the girl; and he sure couldn't do it from that maze of trompings.

He went back to the thicket but there was nothing in there.

There were no dead men anyplace around here. Then he remembered. There wouldn't be, of course—not without they were buried, and he saw no sign that would indicate that.

By the way all those tracks went flying around it was a cinch there had been some powder burned. Nor did Cardigan consider it the least bit likely that this black horse had been the only casualty. Any unhorsed jaspers would have been picked up—probably by the soldiers. Men of the stripe these renegades had sprung from would be too intent on saving their own hides to waste any time on the wounded.

Of course he could always go to the post. If the soldiers had taken any prisoners they were bound to have removed them to Camp Grant for trial. It might be quicker in the long run to go there and question them. It might. But in the meantime Docie . . .

He wouldn't think about that.

He got back on the dun and rode due west a while. The black horse had been heading that way when they'd dropped him. When he reckoned he'd got far enough out to get something Cardigan started another circle, watching particularly for any set of tracks that would seem to be carrying more than the weight of an average rider.

But there weren't any single sets of tracks, none whatever. He made a full circle before he would believe it. The frantic renegades had all spurred west with two or three cavalrymen after each one of them—and they hadn't done any loitering. You could tell by the tracks those cavalrymen were riled.

A guy might as well hunt a needle in a haystack as to try in all that welter of tracks to pick out a set that were toting double weight.

Cardigan's mood wouldn't stand frittering round. With an oath he took after the nearest bunch of tracks.

Three soldiers had spurred after one renegade. The fear had sure been in that feller. He hadn't thought once about hiding his trail. Those cavalry sports must have been too close for the damn scared fool to do any more than spur and sling leather —and he hadn't done that any great while, either.

Half a mile from the scene of the original encounter a carbine bullet had put an end to the chase. You could see where the horse had gone down like a rocket, carried end over end by its own momentum. And there the horse lay, in that catclaw tangle, head twisted under it, too dead to skin.

And there was where the rider had landed, hard, on a shoulder, just beyond that pear clump. There was where he'd clawed to his feet. There was where he'd gone down again, headlong. You could see where the bastard had tried to get up . . . the print of his scuffed left boot toe beside the mark of his bent right knee. Forward of that and deeper, much deeper, was the smooth rounded hollow where his left knee had rested and just to the right of it, complete and sharply defined, was the full spread print of the guy's left hand. You could see where his weight had pressed it deep, the left hand's fingers and that right braced forearm, just before he'd give out and flopped forward on his face.

There was where the soldiers had come up. There was where they'd got off their horses. Here was where they'd stood a bit, watchful, wondering probably if there was any more fight in him, perhaps calling orders, maybe waiting for his answer. One of them had gone forward then. Then the rest had come on and picked the guy up.

Taking him back to the camp, Cardigan thought. Back to stand trial or to be turned over to the civil authorities. Or, maybe, to be buried.

To be buried, he hoped.

With a disgusted grunt he turned the big dun figuring to try his luck on another set; it was all he could do, keep running them down. Then the idea struck him that it might be better to swing north from here in a kind of half circle on the off-chance of picking some more up that way. It would save a lot of time if he could do it, he thought.

So he turned the dun north and wheeled away at a canter, dividing his attention between the ground before him and the surrounding brush. For only a fool would ignore that brush. A wounded sidewinder could be just as deadly as one that hadn't ever shaken his rattles.

The country looked empty as a flung-away hat but he had lived with danger too long a while to put any trust in the look of appearances. Looks were for suckers like that fool of a marshal.

The next tracks he crossed showed but three in the party. The man being chased appeared to have the better horse. He must have had quite a lead and been steadily stretching it because the other gents' tracks frequently swerved far aside in what could only have been hopeful tries to shortcut him. They hadn't been very successful, it looked like, because the chased man's tracks finally straightened into plain departure and, a short distance later, Cardigan came to the place where the soldiers had quit.

There went their tracks angling back toward the bench. One of their horses had been limping badly.

Cardigan's lips showed a grim satisfaction. With that same set look he inspected his rifle, thrust it back in its boot and had a look at his sixgun. These chores attended to he took up the trail.

At four by his shadow Cardigan came to the boulder-strewn course of the dry San Pedro. Here the fugitive's tracks turned into a rutted freight road that came up from the south and probably went to Camp Grant, which lay about thirty miles to the east and north.

Cardigan briefly grinned. It was a cinch the guy wouldn't stay with that road long; Camp Grant would be the last place he'd head for. He'd swung into that road to hide his tracks and he'd done a damn good job of it.

The guy had got hold of his head again and the knowledge turned Cardigan thoughtful. It was time to look spry and he slowed his horse, glad of a chance to breathe the stallion though he knew Jubal was good for many a mile yet; the big dun had once taken him one hundred miles without stopping, and done it in twelve hours.

He sent swift looks up and down the road. The brush was thin along here yet he scanned it carefully, having no desire to fall into an ambush. Satisfied, he gave his attention to the ground along the west edge of the road, pretty well convinced the man would leave from that side—and he did.

Where water, below a ridge, had gullied that edge during some long-forgotten cloudburst the fugitive, making out to be a casual traveler heading south, had eased his horse down into it. Cardigan eased Jubal into it also. Those tracks had been left less than an hour ago.

It was a cinch the guy's horse was about washed up. That wild flight from the troopers hadn't helped it any. By the sign it looked to be going lame.

This could help. It was also bound to increase immeasurably the chance of ambush for the guy, slowed down, might get plenty cute. He was going to be watching his backtrail plenty.

Cardigan stopped the dun and sat turning it over. You could think all you wanted but the facts stayed the same. If he didn't come up with that fellow by dark there was a mighty good chance he wouldn't ever come up with him. The guy knew the country and Cardigan didn't. He would have to chance ambush. He would have to press on, cut down the man's lead and someway close with him before dark fell or he might just as well call it quits right here.

As long as the way remained open Cardigan pushed Jubal Jo along at a lope, but when the chased man's trail began to twist through the brush he was forced to slow down.

Palo verde grew here and the tall-stalked pitahaya thrust up its bloom like a hat on a rifle. The footing became broken and rocky and the dun's shod hoofs made a too-loud clatter as they scrambled up the slope of a shaly ridge. The grease-wood here was far apart, puny. Wolf's candle lifted its gray spiked branches and the renegade's tracks went over the crest and showed as a series of pale contusions dropping down the dusted shelving of the ridge's north flank.

The fugitive's earlier headlong pace had dwindled now to a slow limping shuffle. His horse couldn't last much longer. That crazed panic flight from the men in blue had squandered its strength, poured it out like gold from a drunkard's purse.

Cardigan pulled the dun up with his head cocked, listening, gathering and sifting all the stray vibrations; but nowhere in all that brush-choked yonder could he catch any sound of man or horse. With his bold-featured face still tipped to that listening he considered the buff-colored ground where the slope leveled off down there to the left of him, the fugitive's tracks and the direction they pointed through that yonder tangle of chaparral and pear and the knife-thin gash of a canyon beyond.

It seemed all too empty, too deceptively silent. There should anyway be a few birds twittering down there.

He raked the brush with his eyes and canted his shoulders. If that fellow was down there what was he waiting for—wasn't a rifle shot good enough for him? Had he lost his rifle? Had he run out of cartridges?

There was a way to find out and Cardigan took it.

This was going to be risky but anything he tried was apt to be risky and time was dangerously near to running out. With his face tight and tough Kurt Cardigan nodded and kneed Jubal Jo into motion. As though he were walking on eggs the big dun moved down the slope with his ears cocked. Cardigan's rifle lay across the pommel but he came onto the flat without anything happening.

He said, "Mebbe he ain't here after all," and studied the tracks with a sharpening attention that extended itself to the roundabout brush.

Except over that ridge he had just negotiated there was no other way off this flat but the canyon whose gash showed dead ahead. The ridge and the rising ground that flanked it made of this flat a kind of pocket. The tracks, looking more and more ready to stop, led off toward the canyon by the shortest cut, and they looked to have been made during the last ten minutes.

Was the man still here or had he gone through that canyon?

7

DEAD POSSUM

*H*E GLARED at the tracks, half minded to quit them.

Chasing after this guy had been a damfool business. It had looked good at the start because he'd wanted to save time and catching any of the renegades had looked like the answer. Now he wasn't so sure.

He'd been doing all right till he'd found that dead horse; right then was when his thinkbox had jammed. He should have kept on circling till he'd come onto the tracks of another horse packing double—*those* were the tracks he should have found and followed. Even if he ran this guy down it might do him no good so far as Docie was concerned. The guy might not have any idea where the girl was.

But if he quit this guy now and went back to the bench and then didn't find nothing he'd have to chase down every last track that led out of there. The girl could be a damned grandmaw by that time!

He guessed he had better forget that bench. A bird in the hand was better than no bird. He could at least squeeze the gizzard out of *this* one. It might not get him back that woman but it would sure put the fear into the rest of them buzzards.

That goddam brush didn't look very good.

He'd been shot at plenty and he knew the way lead could sing whizzing past you. It wasn't no sound to stamp and yell boo at.

That guy was probably holed up in this brush right now, setting there grinning with a gun in his hand, just waiting for Cardigan to make a right target.

And all the while time was getting shorter. And time, every tick, was working for the other guy; it wasn't doing anything for Cardigan at all. He had just two choices. He could bust on in and maybe get himself shot or he could turn his horse around and get the hell out of here.

There wasn't nothing complex about it. It was just as damn simple as rolling off a log. It was just a question of which he valued most, the girl—who probably wasn't anywhere around here—or his hide.

He was turning his horse when he suddenly stiffened with his eyes looking like they would roll off his cheekbones.

There, in the brush not ten feet to the right of him, was another set of tracks. Like the ones he had followed they were heading toward the canyon—fresh tracks, too, and heavy looking, like the goddam horse might be packing double.

Cardigan's eyes turned bright and narrow. They raked the brush with a keener interest. His shoulders lifted and a deepened breathing was reflected in the tightness of the shirt across his chest. "I guess," he said to the dun, "we'll go in there," and sent the horse forward without further dalliance.

Midway through the brush of this flat a low wind, wheeling out of the canyon, ran across the tops of the greasewood, waving them, touching his face with the remembered coolness of higher altitudes.

There were a number of second-growth pines up ahead, stunted and stubbly, along the trail just before it turned into the canyon. Pausing again before he reached these, Cardigan, easing around in the saddle, carefully considered the surrounding brush before his glance dropped once more to the deeper indentations left in the dust by the second horse. This horse had gone into the canyon. He was not so sure about the first man's mount—the one he had followed into this country—till he came to where its sign crossed and mingled with the hoofmarks left by the heavy-burdened one.

Cardigan quit stalling then. He rode straight toward the jaws of the canyon. There was nothing in sight from the entrance to where, a couple of hundred yards up ahead, a bulge in the righthand wall cut off all view of what lay beyond it. At that point the sides of the canyon pinched in till the passage looked barely the width of a wagon. It was not much more, he found when he got there, with weathered rock walls rising sheer above him for hundreds of feet to a bright crack of sky that looked miles away.

He could still vaguely pick out the tracks of the horses where they made disturbed areas in the talus that littered the passage floor. He wished he knew the length of this canyon and where this hidden trail would take him.

He rode more slowly now with his rifle booted and a hand near his gun.

The walls, after a while, began to fall back a little. The talus gave way to patches of soil that, as he progressed, became more frequent and of larger extent, muting the dun's footfalls and cooled with the tender green of wild ferns.

A feeling took hold of Cardigan that before the evening advanced much further he might come up with those fellows and be seeing them through gunsmoke.

He watched Jubal's ears with a cold vibration in the pit of his belly. Far as he could tell there was nobody near him but the cold feeling grew and, of a sudden, on an upswing of breeze flowing through the canyon he caught the sharp smell of woodsmoke.

The dun's ears shot forward and he grabbed for its nostrils and had it wheeled clear around before it knew what was happening.

He rode almost back to where the walls narrowed before he took his hand from Jubal's muzzle. He swung quickly down then and stripped off saddle and blanket, bridle and all the rest of his gear, and turned the dun loose on a lass rope. "You stay right here an' no nickerin'—savvy?"

The big dun softly snorted and Cardigan picked up his rifle and started forward on foot, being careful to walk where he'd give the least warning.

It was coolly damp between the high walls and pungent with the aroma of ferns. Berry vines and creepers matted the floor and all the time the smell of woodsmoke got plainer.

Cardigan's face turned tight with the strain of this business and all his nerves were set on hair triggers. When a group of quail drummed from under foot he came within an ace of letting off his rifle.

He stood frozen, glaring, heart hammering madly for a good twenty seconds after the quail were gone. He reckoned he'd better be getting hold of himself.

He made himself stand there till his heart quit pounding, till his breath came natural and the sweat went off him. But he couldn't get the cold feeling out of his belly.

Rounding a bend in the canyon passage he saw a side canyon opening to the left. There was considerable dropped rock about the entrance to it and it looked a choice spot for an ambush.

He approached it gingerly, rifle ready.

Them goddam quail had scared him stiff and he didn't want no more surprises like that.

He took a grip on himself and kept his rifle at the cock in both hands while the woodsmoke smell got stronger and stronger. There was no doubt about it—they were in that side canyon, but he still hadn't heard one dadburned sound.

He reached the first of the rocks and crouched there without hearing anything but the pounding of his heart and that made enough noise to drown out a pump-jack.

He tried to think what he'd better do next. He wanted to get him a look down into that gulch but he was scared to move till he got some sign. Those guys might be a heap closer than you'd think for. They might be no farther than the other side of these rocks and he would be a gone goose if they saw him first.

He wished the hell he'd kept his eyes on those tracks; he'd forgot all about them in the smell of that woodsmoke. He couldn't see any from where he was now—not without getting up. And getting up, by grab, might be mighty unhealthy. It wasn't that he was afraid of them bastards but a mistake right now could be almighty permanent.

Blocks of rock, like young houses, lay scattered all about him, broken by their fall from the cliffs above. He crouched there and sweated, trying to talk himself into boldly sticking his neck out and not managing to move his neck one damn inch. He had the feeling, if he did, he might find himself looking into somebody's pistol.

While he hunkered there trying to screw himself into doing it he suddenly stiffened to the mutter of voices. They were held down and muted but they were voices all right and they were almighty close.

Should he make his play now? They were arguefying now, probably engrossed in their business, and this might be a good time to do it if only he was sure just where they were at.

He gripped his rifle tighter. He guessed he'd better do it now. His patience wouldn't stand much more of this fiddling. And there was the light to be thought of—it wasn't getting no better. If he waited till dark they might get clear away from him. The tempting smells drifting in with that woodsmoke reminded him his gut was getting powerful puny.

He started forward at a crawl, wriggling toward the next boulder.

Crawling, he decided, was for centipedes and Injuns. All the goddam sandburrs and gravel in the country seemed to have shacked up in the lee of that boulder and it felt like his hands and his knees had found most of them. It was a nerve-twisting business what with having all the time to watch out for his rifle, not to stub it full of dirt and not to bank the damn barrel. It didn't leave him much time for any fancy listening and it come over him sudden, them galoots had quit talking.

When he reached the damn boulder he didn't know whether to stick his nose out or not.

It could be just a little unhandy for a feller if some other gun-lugger happened to be doing the same thing.

He crouched there listening but all he could hear was the wind groaning around him.

What the hell were they doing?

Far as he could tell he was the only guy around there and he got to darkly wondering if them birds had pulled out. It made him feel like a sucker and the thought turned him reckless.

There was a way to find out and, scowling blackly, he took it. He grabbed off his hat and stuck his head around the boulder.

The view wasn't improved any great amount to speak of. He found himself staring at a dust-whitened bush that grew up beside the rock a couple feet in front of him. The only way he could look past it was to wriggle on out there.

It wasn't what you'd call a right attractive idea.

The more he thought about it the less he liked it. This rock would stop bullets but the goddam bush wouldn't even stop a fly.

Belly in the dirt, hands and knees sore with burr points, Cardigan knew a sudden sense of bitter outrage. He would sure make them sweat if he ever got hold of them! He'd make them bastards wish they'd never been born! Steal his woman would they? Drag her around like a blanket squaw! By God, if they'd touched one hair of her—

He pulled up in cold panic.

What if she was ugly! What if she was one of them big rawboned wallopers with shovel teeth and a blacksmith's muscle like that long-haired partner old Bill Huxley had drawn that time he'd got high on Merit's Patent Elixir!

God almighty.

Just the thought of such a turn put the cold sweat all over him.

"Jesis!" he said.

He would sure be hooked if he went storming out there to save the old bag and she got her peepers on him. Hell's gilded hinges! It would sure be rough to go to all this trouble and then wind up with some warhorse like that!

Maybe he had better slow down here a little. Maybe he had better go at this thing cautious and get him a look at her before he leaped.

Yeah. That was the ticket. Play it close to the chest. Not do nothing rash till he had got him a look at her. Then, if she ddin't suit him, he could let those bucks have her.

But while he was cheering himself up with that another thought struck him. If she'd been ugly them bastards wouldn't never of run off with her.

He rubbed the palms of his hands on his pantslegs. He put his hat back on and picked up his rifle.

He wriggled on around the rock and inched himself forward till he got his sweating face within a whisper of the bush. He still couldn't see much. The bush grew flat against the ground. Nothing less than a buzzard could see anything through it.

He chewed on his lip and finally stuck his damn head out.

At first all he saw was that wreck of a cabin with the whoppyjawed door hanging wedged on one hinge strap. It was sagged back against the gulch's rocky left shoulder about a hundred yards off like the first good wind would send it kiting into kindling. Then a movement snapped his glance a little farther to the right.

Above a tiny fire a man was crouched facing him. There was a skillet in his hand. A blackened pot was in the embers and beyond, down the gulch a ways, were a couple grazing horses turned loose on hobbles. He didn't see the girl and the second man wasn't in sight.

They were probably in that cabin.

Thought of it made him grind his teeth and his eyes took on a shine that was wicked as he hitched himself around a little and cuddled the rifle snug to his shoulder and drew a bead on the guy by the fire. It was all he could do to keep his squeeze off the trigger.

It wasn't any scruple that stayed his hand. It was the thought of that other guy—the one in the cabin—that kept Kurt Cardigan from pulling that trigger. He meant to get them both and he didn't want to have to camp a week here to do it.

He would wait till that other guy stuck his face out, till he got them both away from that cabin, then he'd cut them down like a couple of snakes.

It made him boil to think of them here with that girl. She was probably scared half out of her wits. Only one thought kept him from going hog wild; they'd been running too fast to work her any mischief—but any fool could tell you what them fellers was after.

The thought did not tend to cool him off any.

Consumed with impatience he lifted the rifle but he lowered it reluctantly without doing anything. The guy with the skillet was only part of this business; there was another guy with him and he aimed to get both of them. It sure burned him up to watch that guy cooking and him starved enough to eat a dog with the hide on.

Then a guy came out of the cabin and Cardigan almost jumped to his feet.

Grave Creek Clanton, the old wrinkle-faced whelp!

Grave Creek Clanton that he'd picked from the gutter and set up in business with a stable at Payson—there was gratitude for you! Taking Cardigan's money and making off with his woman!

When he was able to see straight again, and to think straight, Cardigan knew there was no time for foolishness. That Clanton could shoot the buttons off your shirt. He had jumped more claims and slit more throats than any other bastard in the country; and Cardigan was taking no chances.

He waited till Grave Creek got to the fire. Then he peeled his lips back and let him have it. He flung the barrel over quick and snapped a shot at the other guy.

The bird with the skillet went ass over elbow but Grave Creek Clanton never even staggered. He spun like a cat and started heating his axles. Straight down the gulch he streaked with both legs flying.

Cardigan jumped to his feet and ran out in the open. Grave Creek was dashing down the gulch full tilt, doing his damnedest to get into the trees. Cardigan dropped to a knee and crashed a couple slugs after him. The second one got him and he went down like a duck. He flopped around on the ground like a wolf with its throat cut.

Cardigan got up and worked the lever of his rifle.

With a fresh shell under the hammer he felt better. He even felt a little sorry for the bastard now. That had always been his trouble, too much pity, too much softness.

He was halfway down to where he'd seen Clanton flopping when the sidewinder reared right up on his hunkers with a gun in each fist and both of them spitting.

Something belted the brim of Cardigan's bonnet. Something jerked at his vest, cut his holster plumb off. Then he went down on his belly and never quit firing till his rifle was empty.

When the smoke cleared away Grave Creek Clanton wasn't moving. He was flat on his back and he wasn't playing possum.

8

AN OLD THIEF GOES HOME

*B*UT CARDIGAN was all through playing Good Samaritan.

He guessed he would go on up to the cabin and get that girl cut loose of her ropes and maybe after that, if he got to feeling like it, he would come back down here and plant these jaspers.

He started for the shack but his knees got to shaking so bad he couldn't make it. He got down on the ground and shook and sweat till his stomach muscles came out of their tangle and he was able to draw a full breath without retching.

Evening's lonesome light was filling this gulch and he looked at the shack but didn't put any strain on himself getting over there.

He had to get a couple things straightened out in his mind first. Like whether he had ought to fetch the girl or not. Of course if they'd left her tied up—and he reckoned they had or she'd been out before this—he guessed he would have to; but right now the idea of having him a woman lacked considerable of being as attractive as it had. He didn't know what the hell had come over him but he couldn't get worked up over that woman for sour apples. Not even the idea of crawling in bed with her seemed worth a second thought the way he felt right now.

He reckoned maybe he'd feel different after he got some grub in him. Been a powerful long while since he'd sunk his molars in a good piece of cow flesh and, one thought naturally leading to another, it came to him one of them guys had been cooking.

He got up with a groan and moseyed over to the fire.

As a matter of precaution he looked the cooker over first. But there was no need to worry about that guy. A little wrinkled-up wart with a face like a bullfinch, he had caught Kurt's slug square between the eyes.

Cardigan looked at him and grunted. Then his glance found the skillet. A piece of burned sow bosom was stuck to its bottom. He cut it loose with his knife and bit him off a sample. He picked up the smoke-sooted pot from the ashes and found it half full of good black java which slid down mighty easy.

He finished the pork and poked around some more but, except for the frijoles strewed all over the ground, there were no further eatables anyplace in sight. Looked like these cabrones had been living off cut straw and molasses. Guessed the road agent business wasn't paying off no better these days than raising cattle.

With a disgusted grunt he finally headed for the cabin. Might as well see what kind of a card he'd been drawing to, but he sure wished again he'd never written that letter.

Time he reached the sagged door he was sweating like a nigger. He was shaking in his boots like a boghole rider after tailing twenty steers. He had to get behind and shove himself to get him to the door and he damn near bolted when he heard a stifled groan.

"Jesis!" he said, and couldn't turn a finger.

If that had come from a woman he didn't want any part of her.

Like a wolf in a trap he stood there with his hackles up, scarcely even breathing so intently was he listening. Gray gloom crept through the gulch and thickened and all he could hear was the bumping of his heart.

He finally lifted a hand and found it frozen to his rifle. He wanted to laugh but his mouth wouldn't shape it.

What the hell was in that cabin?

With an almighty care he set his rifle against the wall. With an equal stealth he eased the pistol from his trousers where he was being forced to pack it on account of Grave Creek Clanton.

The inside of that cabin was black as a stack of stovelids.

He looked a long while before he decided to go in there. He felt prominent as a new saloon in a church district and it took all the strength of his entire body to lift one foot and put it down across that doorstep. The floor gave out a banshee wail and his eyes plunged into the blackness wildly. He damn near choked the grip off his pistol but nothing happened.

He took a ragged breath.

He gnawed at his lip and felt sweat collect in the palms of his hands and then, off in a corner, there was a kind of hoarse breathing; and he tipped up his gun and said: "Strike a light!"

He half expected the blackness to explode in a gun flash but nothing at all happened. No one moved. No sound came out of that tight black silence and Cardigan snarled: "Strike a light, by God, or I'll let you have it!"

The only answer he got was a faint repetition of that labored breathing. Then a tired sigh came from the corner. "You'd . . . be wastin' your lead," a man's voice said faintly. "I ain't got much more than . . . a couple breaths left."

Cardigan's eyes raked the gloom suspiciously.

"Where you at?"

"Over here."

"I could figure out that much."

"I'm . . . in the bunk," the man said, so low Kurt had to lean forward to hear him.

He was thinking to himself he'd better watch this fellow. He might of lost his gun and this could all be a trick to get Kurt over there. He might be crouched with a club. He might have hold of a knife.

Cardigan licked his lips. "What's the matter with you?"

"Hell . . . I'm all shot t' pieces." The labored gasp of his breathing became suddenly frantic and he cried in a half-strangled voice: "It's so goddam black!" And then, weakly: "Are you there, Art?"

"I'm right here," Cardigan said. He moved forward a little, all his senses alert for the first sign of treachery. "Where's the girl?"

The guy didn't answer. There wasn't any sound but the man's terrible breathing. Cardigan, listening into that blackness, heard the slats of the bunk creak. "Mother!" the man cried brokenly, but Cardigan kept a tight hold on his pistol.

"Where's the girl?" he repeated, but all the breath seemed to be running out of the man.

With a smothered curse Cardigan plowed through the dark till his knees brought up against the side of the bunk.

He drew back the hammer of his gun and struck a match. The light raveled down across the man on the bunk. He'd been shot all right—he was a hell of a sight. His beard-stubbled cheeks were the color of chalk.

His eyes fluttered open. "You . . . you still there, pard?"

Cardigan, scowling, put the pistol away. He reached down a hand to the man's bony shoulder. "What'd you do with the girl?"

The man didn't answer. He seemed too far gone even to

notice the light and it was obviously only a matter of moments now.

"The girl!" Cardigan said. "What'd you do with the girl?"

"Girl . . . Oh! Soldiers got her—got Benny an' Snell. Clanton turned her . . . loose when they dropped his horse. Figured that might stop 'em, but . . . Pull my boots off, will you?"

The match burned out and Cardigan dropped it. He bent over, hating it, and pulled the guy's boots off.

"Don't," the man pleaded, "tell Mother I . . . died like this."

"Hell," Cardigan said, "what you need's a drink—"

"Hold . . . hold my hand will you, pardner?"

Cardigan took the cold hand.

It seemed to please the guy someway. Another of those terrible sighs welled out of him. "Could"—the cracked voice took on a wistful note—"could you sing me a . . . hymn?"

"Well, Jesis Christ!" Cardigan said, and stopped. After all, the poor bastard was just about done for. It was little enough anyone could do for him. "What about—" He scowled a moment, trying to think of one.

"Somethin' with Mother. . . ." The man muttered faintly.

Cardigan swallowed a couple of times to get the sow belly out of his gullet. He could damn well do with a drink himself. He cleared his throat self-consciously and sang in a husky baritone:

> "After the roundup is over,
>   after the shippin' is done
> I'm going to see my mother
>   before my money's all gone.
> My mother's heart is breakin',
>   breakin' for me that is all;
> An' with God's help I'll see her
>   when the work is done this fall.
>
> " 'Twas along in the shank of the evenin'
>   this boy went out to stand guard,
> The wind was blowin' fiercely
>   an' the rain was fallin' hard.

> The cattle they got frightened
> an' ran in mad stampede;
> Poor boy, he tried to head them—"

The man's cold hand squeezed Cardigan's fingers. "Tell her that," he whispered, and his grip fell away.

Kurt Cardigan reached up and pulled off his hat.

"God damn it," he said, and got out of there.

9

SUNDRY MATTERS OF MOMENT

*W*HEN THINGS got too tough in Nogales, Stella Mae Larpin, who had once been a stock broker's darling, threw her clothes in a bag and took the next stage for Tucson. There was nothing for her in Nogales anyway; all the loose jack had gone to Cananea and a girl in her business had things tough enough without competition from Mexican chippies. All her favorite johns had run out on her and she was tired of the same old sevens and eights.

Tucson, she'd found, was a big improvement. Things really hummed on Meyer Street and the sports who patronized Long Tooth Emma's were strictly on the up and up and never tried to hand you any crap about charging it.

Long Tooth Emma kept the squirreliest place. You never would have guessed the old bag was a madam. She dressed like something out of Godey's Lady Book and used the most refined language Stella Mae had ever heard. She had real class and no mistake about it.

Her place was right in the heart of town, a big old adobe smack up against the bank. It was the flossiest joint outside of Dodge City and its Sunday Chicken Dinners were the talk of the town. It had been a hotel and a lot of folks still thought it one—a thought Miss Emma was happy to cultivate. The old lobby was used as a sitting room with a bar at one end and a melodeon at the other and almost any evening you could find six or eight of the town's solid citizens taking their rest there and auguring politics, the price of beef or which horse was going to win the race next Sunday. Most of the horses around Tucson were "short" horses—Doc Gallaway called them "gamblers' horses" and he sure had the right of it, considering the betting.

After scratching for a living like she had in Nogales, Stella Mae found life at Miss Emma's like a dream. It was the softest berth she had ever got into but there was times when all the quiet and refinement made her want to jerk her hair out and tear around screaming. Navajo rugs on the polished floors, serapes on the walls, and framed oil paintings of range life and horses and pine-covered hills. That kind of stuff could get on your nerves and make you wish, by God, you hadn't ever been born—particular when Charlie sat down at the melodeon and played that piece about the tender apple blossom.

Top Hat Charlie was an English remittance man who'd been shipped to Arizona to die with TB. He didn't work for Emma but ran a faro bank at the Gold Plate Saloon and had the reputation of being the fastest dealer in the West. He had the airs and appearance of a Princeton man and was one of the few high rollers who had the good sense to stay away from booze. And was damned good-looking in a cold, reserved way, but the craziest guy she had ever run into. Every time he sat himself down at the melodeon it was to play some dirge like that tender apple blossom and his taste in women was confined to Mexicanas.

The guy Stella Mae could really have gone for was a yellow-haired rancher by the name of Kurt Cardigan. The guy really got you. He wasn't a regular and most of the time he would just drop around and wag his jaw with Miss Emma or listen to the gab of the johns at the bar. Sometimes you wouldn't see him for months at a whack, but he sure was a sport and when he went on a tear he would throw his jack around just like it was washers sawed off a lead pipe.

Would she ever forget the time he'd dragged her off shopping? Been figuring to fix up his house, he'd said, and wanted her opinion on what junk to get and how to arrange it. He'd drawn her some diagrams and talked the thing over till she could just about see the place with her eyes shut. It had been fun at first picking out that stuff and seeing the looks on the shopkeepers' faces; it had been a peck of fun till it had suddenly come over her what her kind of woman had on tap to look forward to. Ever since that time she'd had just one ambition: to get herself a stake while the getting was good.

That Kurt was a card and no getting around it but anyone could see he'd never fall for a woman. He would kid with them all and make a pass when it pleased him but you just couldn't picture the guy in double harness. She remembered that time they'd gone swimming in the Santa Cruz. . . .

Thoughts of Kurt Cardigan always made her restless but she wasn't the kind to beat her head against a wall. Some things you could get and some you couldn't. The smart thing to do was to get what you could and the john she was putting her best foot forward for was Cardigan's range boss, Curly Lahr. With his mop of red hair and his saturnine eyes he wasn't a man to whom laughter came easy and he wasn't any favorite with the girls at Miss Emma's. But Stella Mae reckoned she had got Lahr figured and always made out like she was glad to see him. He wasn't free and easy like his boss and sometimes, in a clinch, he would get pretty rough. But Stella Mae could make out to put up with a powerful lot if it looked like getting her what she was after.

She was after security, but not that alone.

She had no intention of selling herself short and reaching out for a meal ticket when more could be had by playing her cards right. A rolling stone, to be sure, might gather no moss but it was bound to acquire a certain amount of polish, and if her three years of rolling around with men had left her few illusions there had been compensations of more practical value.

She wasn't thinking of the experience those years had given her but rather of the insight that had come as result of it. Stella Mae had always figured she could add two and two; she could add three and two now and make it come out five.

She knew men and, in the aggregate, precious little good of them. Some were worse than others but at the bottom of them all there was a hard core of selfishness that influenced all their actions.

This was knowledge and an asset, all you had to do was use it.

Thinking of the two men, Cardigan and his range boss, she had analyzed the things she saw and settled on the latter. Cardigan was fun to be with. He possessed a certain attraction and a considerable reputation; he had land and cows and horses, a standing in the community not enjoyed by Curly Lahr. But she had watched him with that yellow horse and, tough as big Kurt Cardigan was, she sensed in him a soft streak. It took a man as hard as nails to get anyplace in this country. Any softness was a weakness and someday that weakness would catch him out.

In the taciturn Curly Lahr she saw a means of reaching her goal. In the redheaded, green-eyed ranch boss Stella Mae recognized, beneath his dour exterior, a burning ambition that would never let the man rest as the hired hand of another.

Here was a man to be reckoned with.

Bone and brawn might tame this country but bone and brawn would be little likely to lay at her feet those things that Stella Mae secretly craved. Outwardly Cardigan was plenty tough but Lahr was tough inside and out. Right away she had sensed the guile in his nature, the hidden craft, the drive of the man. It seemed strange he had managed to fool Kurt so long; she had guessed what he was up to within a week of meeting him. Cardigan's ambition was tempered with caution; Lahr didn't know the meaning of the word. It wasn't caution that was holding Lahr back but only plain horse sense—good judgment; he was biding his time; merely waiting for the break.

She didn't know his background or need to. She saw all she needed in the man himself. His driving hunger was fused with subtlety and a sharp and corrosive discernment. He knew what he wanted and she'd have bet every stitch she had on her that he saw how to go about getting it.

Curly Lahr wanted power and when he ruled this country she aimed to have a share in the spoils he'd come into.

Ed Reagan, proprietor of the Lone Star Livery, couldn't get his mind properly fixed on his card game after that dude had gone off with Kurt Cardigan. There was something about that business that was fishy and his thoughts kept trying to turn up what it was.

In the first place the danged dude hadn't talked enough. Even counting the bad news he was supposed to have received it still wasn't natural he should be so close-mouthed. Most of the dudes Ed had ever met up with had been as long on talk as they were short on savvy.

Ed was glad when his friend said he guessed he'd have to go.

Afterwards when Reagan had the place to himself he didn't clean the stalls as he'd intended doing; instead he tipped back his chair in the shade of the entrance and tried to figure out what had stirred this unrest that was jumping around in him.

Perhaps the feeling he had was compounded of several things.

He considered that a while and after a bit he nodded. Why, for instance, had Cardigan been in such a sweat?

What was it he'd said now? That the dude needn't worry about Injuns, that Cardigan himself would be going through with him. That he wasn't delivering no horses—that he was riding up there to look for the stage.

And why should Kurt Cardigan care about the stage?

That was queer in itself when you stopped to consider it— almost as queer as him offering explanations. It wasn't like Cardigan to ever explain anything.

Yet Cardigan had told him the dude was in a hurry, that he'd had bad news and had to get to El Paso. The dude had looked, right enough, like he'd had bad news but he hadn't looked to Ed to be in much of a hurry. It was Kurt all the time that had been trying to rush things, Kurt who'd suggested his speediest horses, Kurt who had helped him to get the mare ready and had paid the whole cost right out of his own pocket.

It had looked uncommon strange to Ed Reagan.

He had known Kurt Cardigan for upwards of five years and never before had he observed the big rancher to show as much lather over anybody else.

"By crackey," Ed said, getting out of his chair, "I believe I'll jest take me a little walk uptown."

He stopped by the barber shop and stuck his head in the door. "Seen Cardigan around?"

"Yeah," the barber said, "but he ain't here now. Had some words with Esparza an' rode off towards the Pass."

So he'd had words with Esparza.

Reagan turned that over and went across to the stage office. "Joe," he said, with his elbows on the counter, "was Cardigan expectin' anything on that stage?"

The agent glanced up and considered him briefly. He brushed the damp hair back away from his forehead. "He didn't say, Ed."

Reagan rasped his gray jowls. "Did he . . . did he seem a-tall put out account it hadn't got in?"

The stage agent looked a long while at his desk top. He puffed out his cheeks and finally picked up his pen again. "Afraid I can't answer that question, Ed."

"But he musta said *some*thin'!"

"You didn't hear it from me."

Reagan stared and then snorted.

Outside in the burning glare of the sun his glance swung over the drowsing town and picked up the dust-yellow ribbon of road where it crawled through the heat on its climb toward the Pass. No stage and no riders anywhere on it. The desert lay blistering in its infinite hush and a spiralling dust devil tossed its brown breath across the shimmering blue of the far-away mountains. Somewhere out there that dude and Cardigan were riding. . . .

With a grunt Ed Reagan bent his steps past the bank and past the entrance to Miss Emma's and turned into the Oasis House. At the desk Frank Esparza stood beside the stooped clerk. They both looked at Reagan and neither man spoke.

Reagan vaguely felt a little uncomfortable and wondered

if the pair had been talking about him. He said, "Looks like them 'Paches musta grabbed that stage," and the clerk gloomily nodded.

"Does sorta look that way," the marshal said and, with a thoughtful tug at his mustache, walked out.

Reagan peered after him. Then he turned to the clerk. "You got a dude stayin' here?"

"Funny you should ask that. Frank just asked me the same damn thing."

"Well," Reagan said, "I was just kinda curious."

"So was Frank. The guy's been here three days an' no one said a word about him. Now—"

"What sort of lookin' feller is he?"

"Kinda short an' fat. Wears a stiff hat an' smokes black cigars. Sunburnt—"

"That's the guy," Reagan said. "What name does he go by?"

"Accordin' to the book his name is Sam Sollantsy. What's he done—stuck up the bank?"

"S'far as I know he ain't done nothin'. I was—"

"Yeah. Just curious. You an' the marshal. I'm gettin' curious myself. In fact, I'm gettin' *damn* curious. Somebody shoot him?"

"No," Reagan said. "It's just that . . . Well, I'll tell you. He come into my place a while ago an' bought a horse."

"Lots of— Oh. Yeah," the clerk said, looking carefully at Reagan. "What'd he want a horse for?"

"There was some talk of El Paso. Seems he'd had some bad news an' had to hit out—"

"Must of been damn sudden," the clerk said, scowling.

"What I thought," declared Reagan, nodding. "Takin' off acrost the desert in all this heat. Of course—" Reagan had a sudden hunch not to bring Cardigan into this, and he let the rest trail off, spreading his hands with a shrug. "Didn't hop his bill, did he?"

"I'll take care of that," the clerk told him, frowning.

Reagan dragged his spurs back out onto the porch. The trapped heat off the street was like a breath from a furnace.

A man moved from the wall and went down the steps with him.

"Happened to hear your remarks about that drummer," Esparza said. "Did he tell you himself he had to go to El Paso?"

"Well, not in so many words, but—" Reagan began to wish suddenly he had kept his nose out of this. "That seemed to be the idea," he said lamely.

"Where'd he get this bad news you mentioned?"

"He didn't say."

"What *did* he say?"

"Well, to tell you the truth he didn't say much of anythin'."

"Did he give you the notion he might be runnin' from something?"

Reagan wiped his forehead. "I can't say that he did."

"Looks damn peculiar. What did Cardigan want?"

Reagan stopped stalk still. "Cardigan?" He had to moisten his lips twice to get the one word out.

"He was down to your place wasn't he?"

"Sure he was down to my place," Reagan said, not liking the way Frank Esparza was eyeing him.

"Well?" Esparza said.

"I don't get the connection. He drops in at my place whenever it suits him—"

"He dropped in with the dude."

"Now you mention it," Reagan said carefully, "I guess he did. What about it?"

"How long you known Cardigan?"

Reagan wished more than ever he had kept his nose out of this. He didn't know where this talk was being herded but he had a strong hunch that being a party to any talk inimical to Cardigan could be mighty unpleasant if the matter ever happened to be brought to Kurt's attention.

There'd been occasions in the past to amply justify this feeling. Take the case of Val Jones that had packed the star at Paradise. Been pretty well liked when he'd been cowboying for the Cherrycows, a little wild maybe, perhaps a little too ready to reach for his shooting-iron. In a puncher those penchants had aroused no great amount of animus, but he had fetched both failings to his job as town marshal and a lot of people up there thought him prone to exceed his duty. Cardigan had breezed into town with Curly Lahr one day and inside of ten minutes Marshal Jones had jumped him. Nobody ever had quite got the straight of it but Val was said to have used some rough language and wound up his insults by demanding Kurt's gun. Lahr had afterwards said he was afraid there'd be gunplay. He had rushed up behind Kurt and clapped both arms around him just as Cardigan had slid his gun from leather. There had been some confusion, probably mostly in the minds of those who had seen it, but the gun had been discharged and when the smoke cleared away Val Jones had been dead with a hole blown plumb through him.

The coroner's jury had turned Kurt loose and no one had called it a miscarriage of justice, but there you were. Val Jones was plenty *corpus* and no two ways about it.

Reagan took off his hat and mopped his bald head industriously. "What was that you was sayin'?"

"I said how long you known Cardigan?"

"Well, let's see . . . four-five years."

"Bought any of his horses?"

"I've bought a few off an' on."

"Suit you all right did they?"

"They was worth what he charged me if that's what you're gettin' at."

The marshal pushed out his lips. "You ever been out there?"

"Can't say that I hev."

"Well, these horses you've bought—come pretty cheap did they?"

Reagan turned it over.

"In my line of business you got to watch all the angles. Most of the time I buy from fellers that ain't got no reg'lar market for their stuff, fellers in the sticks, guys that ain't got no reason to look fer fancy prices. When I wanta git good ones I buy 'em from Cardigan."

"Think he raises pretty good stuff do you?"

"When you git a hoss from Cardigan you know it'll git the job done."

"When he came into your place with that dude," Esparza said, "what were they talkin' about?"

"Since you ask me, I didn't hear 'em talk about anythin'."

"When they headed for your place," Esparza said, "they were together."

"Look—" Reagan grumbled, "it's too damn hot to stand out here chinnin'. Let's go down to the stable—time I was gettin' back anyway."

They turned toward the livery without further talk, the marshal appearing thoughtful, Reagan thinking, too.

Reagan dropped into a chair at his desk and got out his handkerchief and mopped his face again. "If we don't git rain soon we'll forgit what water looks like outside of a pail or dipper."

The marshal said bluntly, "When Cardigan and this drummer headed for your place they were together."

"All right," Reagan said. "I ain't arguin' about it. So what if they was? I can't see where all this gabbin' is gettin' us."

"When two gents walk together they most generally talk some. You say they didn't talk much after they got here. Now it caught at my attention they didn't do much talkin' on the way down here, either."

"Well," Reagan said, squirming around in his chair, "you an' me didn't f' that matter. Mebbe they jest happened to meet up with each other. The dude had got bad news—he was in a big hurry t' git to El Paso. He sees Kurt Cardigan, goes dashin' up to him. 'Where kin I git a hoss?' he says. Prob-'ly Cardigan says, 'Why'n't you try the livery?' an' brings the guy down here."

"It could've happened that way," the marshal conceded, but not as though he put any stock in it. "Suppose you tell me what happened when they got there."

"I already told you. Nothin' happened. I sold the guy a hoss."

Esparza looked at him.

Reagan mopped his face. His hand got to fiddling with the

papers on his desk and he picked one up and dropped it into the drawer.

The silence piled up. So did the film of sweat that beaded Reagan's forehead.

The marshal considered him. When he finally spoke it was in the measured language of Ed Reagan's generation. There was a broad streak of tolerance running through the casual words; there was a sadness in them too and, underlying all, there was a hard core of pressure that was not to be ignored.

"This town is changin', Ed. Different crowd taking over. Used to be when a gun went off no one paid much notice. If a man was dead they buried him. Now they want to know all about it, all the little whys and wherefors. You might say I'm a sign of the changin' times. I'm the watchdog they've hired to make sure their notions are properly respected, I'm the bloodhound they feed to find out the answers. Kind of lonesome job, all things considered. But they don't care about that—they don't care about me or about town limits or any other thing. When you sum it up all they want is protection.

"That's all *you* want. The right to eat an' live and run your life as best suits you. You're a part of this, Ed. You pay part of the taxes. You want to share in the things my job makes practical. But it doesn't end there. The knife cuts both ways. When I took this job I told you boys that. I can handle my end. I can keep the wolves down but I can't give you protection if I don't have your confidence."

Reagan stirred in his chair, scrubbed a hand across his jowls. "Well," he said testily, "what're you gettin' at?"

"Just this. When I go to a taxpayer for information I like to feel I'm getting it."

Color touched the stableman's cheeks, and then anger. "I told you—"

"It's the part you ain't told me that I'm waitin' to hear. Somethin' happened in this stable, somethin' connected with that dude or you wouldn't of gone up there askin' about him."

"I thought the guy was loco goin' off in this heat!"

"Suppose you told him about those Injuns—"

"Course I told him about 'em!"

"It takes a mighty brash dude to thumb his nose at Apaches."

Reagan shut his mouth.

"You're holdin' something back, Ed. There's doubt workin' through you and a lot of suspicion. A marshal generally knows when a man is feelin' jumpy."

He stopped long enough to get out his pipe and he sat a moment holding it, then put it away.

He looked at Reagan steadily. "It takes a mighty brave man or a mighty anxious one to get on a horse an' cross that desert right now. You say it was bad news that made him clear out of here but where would he get it?"

He got up and put his hat on. "It sticks out a mile, Ed."

"What does?"

"The part you ain't mentioned. The part about Cardigan."

10

HIDDEN MANEUVERS

COMING OUT of the shack Cardigan clapped on his hat and his narrowing glance, intensely aware of that shape by the fire, turned edgy and angrily filled with resentment.

Death was so goddam final!

He raked a bitter glance through the roundabout shadows.

It was almost full dark and the wind tumbling down off the rimrocks was as cold to the touch as a bartender's heart. It was generally that way out here on the desert; when the sun went down the air cooled quickly, but never had its cold so got into him before. He pulled the scarf closer about his neck and didn't much like the feel of that either.

He didn't know what the hell ailed him. He tried to pull himself together. He was hungry, that was all. Dog tired and bone weary. He couldn't understand such weariness; he'd been tired before but his knees hadn't shook.

He swore in a disturbed uneasy fashion and caught up his rifle and set off up the canyon. Then he slowed down and stopped while he rolled up a smoke. But the thing had no taste and he threw it away, entirely dissatisfied. Unrest churned through him like wind through a hayfield and he clenched his jaws like he would grind off the cups of every tooth in his head.

If only he never had written that woman!

There was the start of this, the black root of everything. No use to blame Krailor or Rickven's daughter—with his own damn hand he had written that letter.

No harm, he had thought, in just writing a letter. . . .

He cursed, scowling blackly.

The cards were dealt now and he would have to play the hand out, like it or not. But he couldn't help thinking what a nizzy he had been. Kid stuff, by grab—and him a growed man!

"Love 'em all you feel like but never lug 'em home." That was what he'd told the boys, and he had made it stick. It was just plain hoss sense and had worked out well for them. And here he was now all set to break his own commandments.

But he couldn't back out now; by this time Docie would be waiting at the fort—probably swinging her jaw in forty directions. Telling that nizzy old gaffer of a post commander all about how she had come here to marry Cardigan. A fine kettle of fish. He had always made out to be a man of his word and if he turned her down now every tongue in that goddam fort would start wagging!

Pride aside, he couldn't afford it. He was selling the cavalry a heap too many horses to get the colonel riled up over any play like that. Let that dimwit ever get it into his head that Cardigan's word wasn't something you could bank on, there wasn't no telling where this deal might wind up. Maybe he had ought to pull out of this business. No matter how well a man covered his tracks there was always the chance of a slip-up; and the way things were going of late, by godfreys, it behooved a man to figure mighty careful.

There were currents in Cardigan, wheels within wheels. He'd come into this country to make his stake and had got a pretty fair start on it; not so good a start, however, that he could relish any thought of pulling out now. What he was doing, he told himself, was not a bit worse than plenty of other guys—some of whom were right important gents in this country, and respected.

There was a wild streak in him and a soft streak, too, and these were compounded by the stubbornness bequeathed him by a long line of forebears who'd gone after what they wanted. What, for instance, was the difference between a banker foreclosing on some poor bastard's outfit and a guy who merely lifted three or four of his horses? To Cardigan it seemed a simple matter of degree and, in this light, all the odds were with the latter. There were unwritten rules in this country and so long as you played by these rules it was nobody's business but your own how you lived.

The rules were flexible enough to suit Cardigan's purpose. Gamblers, for example, were expected to try and fleece you; if you fleeced them instead, folks laughed and slapped your back. When they fleeced you you were considered a sucker. If you caught a gambler cheating you were privileged to shoot him and no one thought the worse of either of you for it. If you got shot yourself that was all right too, unless your friends cared to make something of it.

Rumor might paint a man black as forty stovelids—might call him a bandit, a rustler or stage-robber, but he was seldom accused or treated as one until he grew so bold or so careless that somebody got the deadwood on him. When that happened, if the guy had any wheels in his think-box, he cut his stick in a hurry and removed to calmer parts.

If he was able.

Cardigan grunted.

Most of them were. As a matter of insurance most of those operating outside of the law had friends scattered around in likely places who would give them the word before anything happened.

Cardigan hadn't bothered to make friends. Why split the profit? he had asked himself; it assayed low enough after splitting with your men. He never went out of his way to hunt trouble but he never had tried to make folks beholden to him. He had preferred, instead, to keep his trap shut and play his hand as he found it.

He was beginning to realize the shortcomings of this method.

Too many things were piling up on him. Self-sufficiency was fine if a man could afford it, but how many could?

It was a startling thought which had never before occurred to him. He was a man who had learned to live by his wits, to absorb impressions as a sponge sucks up water, to make his decisions on stray words and gestures, on the shades of expression flitting through a man's eyes, on marks in the dust and inexplicable feelings. And the whole feeling of this country in the last few hours was bothering him.

He paused to shape a smoke, still thinking about it. The paper tore in his fingers and he flung it away while his thoughts got blacker and blacker.

It was writing that letter that had got it all started. If he hadn't written that St. Louis woman he would never have gone to meet that stage. If he hadn't been stewin about the damn stage he'd of taken a smoother line with that drummer. If he hadn't got tangled up with the dude he'd of hunted the stage right after he'd eaten and would have had no call to swap words with the marshal. Or to of done all that jawin in front of Ed Reagan. Or to have found himself needing to go on to Camp Grant when all of his druthers would have turned him straight home.

Though a horse thief could swing just as high as trees grew, there was one thing from which Kurt could still take comfort. He might look no better in the eyes of the law but it could not be said that his depredations had ever worked a real hardship on anyone. He didn't stick up banks, rob stages or roll drunks; he confined his thievery strictly to horses and the men he stole from could afford it.

At ranch headquarters the crippled cook, Hennessy, looked up from the bench where he'd been cutting up spuds and watched Curly Lahr get off a lathered horse. It was three o'clock in the afternoon, a peculiar time for a range boss to be showing up at headquarters.

Lahr tossed his reins and clanked into the shade with his sun-ruddied cheeks about as genial as a bulldog's. "Kurt back yet?"

"Ain't seen 'im."

Lahr scowled a while, silent. "You can slack off on that grub," he said then, taking off his hat and thumbing the sweat from his eyes. "Crew won't be in fer a long time yet —they're bringin' in a bunch we picked up around Florence."

"Ain't that gettin' a little mite close?" the cook said.

The range boss' eyes slammed into him—hard. "This cookin' job suit you?"

Hennessy sat there a moment. "I've done things I like better," he said finally, and got up and dippered water into the kettle of spuds. He poured a slug into himself and limped back.

"Kurt's been gone quite a spell. Three days," Lahr said, "an' not a word outa him."

Hennessy wiped off his knife on a pantsleg. "He coulda gone on a bender—"

"He ain't doin' no bendin' in Tucson—I looked."

The cook said worriedly, "You don't reckon that damn yeller stud—"

Lahr made a noise with his mouth and sat down. "You tell me. Here's what he done, near as I can make out. He rode that dun into town an' hitched across from the stage office, hangin' round there all mornin'. Fed his face at Jelks' hash house an' then him an' some coffee drummer went down t' Reagan's stable. The drummer got a horse an' took the road fer El Paso.

"Comin' back from the livery Cardigan stopped in front

of Warner's an' Esparza come off the porch an' swapped talk
with him. Then Kurt climbs on to that yeller stud-hoss an' hits
off across that blisterin' desert. That make any sense t' you?"

Hennessy imbedded his knife in the bench. "What the hell
would he talk about with Frank Esparza?"

"That," Lahr said, "is what *I* want to know."

"By cripes," Hennessy said, "I don't like it! That marshal
was out here this mornin' nosin' round . . ."

"Three days ago Kurt talks to him; today he comes out
here—"

"To look at some horses!"

They considered each other across a lengthening silence.

Lahr's narrowed eyes watched the corrosive of his thought
darkly spread through the crippled cook. He said at last, very
softly, "Which ones did you show him?"

"Didn't show 'im any—wasn't nothin' up but them geldin's
in the corral there. I told him t' come back when the boss
was t' home."

"An' he rode off then?"

"Not right then. Wanted t' know 'f it would be all right
fer him t' go out an' look around. I told him he could look if
he wanted but he wouldn't see much outside of some young
stuff that wasn't quite ready t' be put t' work yet."

Hennessy scrubbed the back of a hand across his whisk-
ered cheeks and, above that hand, his questioning eyes
quartered Lahr's face with a need for knowledge. He said:
"Esparza asked a funny thing then. Wanted t' know if we
been losin' much stock. Now why would he be askin' a thing
like that?"

Lahr's laugh was short. "Didn't you jest say yourself you
thought Florence was close? Hell! We been nickin' outfits
a heap closer than that; an' it ain't been Kurt—it's been *me*
that's had t' take these damn close-in bunches."

It looked for a bit as though the bait would go untasted;
then the cook got up and said dustily: "Why?"

Lahr knew mighty well what the man was asking but he
chose to misread the cook's plain question.

"Hell's fire!" he scowled. "Why's a man do *any*thing round

this spread? You ought t' know by now who gives out the orders. Alls *I* do is pass 'em along—an' ramrod 'em through!" he added bitterly.

They were silent then with the cook plainly thinking and making hard work of it. But Lahr, knowing through long study when to keep his mouth shut, stared glumly down at his boots and said nothing. He had cast his seed on fertile ground and was satisfied to let it grow without prodding.

Hennessy said at last, darkly. "Mebbe I better cut loose of this outfit."

"The rats," Lahr murmured, "are always first t' quit ship."

The cook wheeled his head with a sullen stare. "You hankerin' t' hev your neck stretched?"

Lahr shrugged.

Hennessy snorted. "When a man starts stealin' from his neighbors he's jest out-an' out askin' t' git his neck stretched. I'm gittin' out! Any time you find me dancin' on air it'll be fer a heap better reason than helpin' t' stuff dollars into someone else's pockets!"

Lahr said contemptuously, "You churn air like a windmill but what does it amount to? Blowin' off steam don't profit a màn nothin'. Your guts is like quicksand—'f you had any bottom you'd do somethin' about it."

The cook came off the bench with his teeth bared but Lahr didn't even turn his head to look at him. He said, "It's mostly like that with these guys that talk big. You don't hear me soundin' off, do you? I don't like to be suckered no better'n the next but you don't hear me runnin' off at the mouth about it. An' you won't. I leave all the runnin' fer fellers like you."

It was almost more than Hennessy could take. Anger had chased all the fright from his features and outrage was painting brash pictures in his head, but some vestige of caution still was in him and it finally set him back down on the bench.

Lahr let him glower for a while and then said, "I had this thing pegged the day he rode out of here. Findin' out he had that talk with the marshal an' now hearin' from you that Esparza's been out here only shows me the proof of what I'd already figured."

"Well?" Hennessy growled.

"We piled up this dough on a kind of pardnership basis, Kurt t' take the bigger share for the plannin' an' bossin', but with each of us due for a good-sized cut. We been free to draw on ours anytime but, mostly, we've just let it pile up with his. We—"

"Hell, I know all that!"

"Know how much you got comin'?"

"I kin figger it out—I know I got plenty," the cook said irascibly.

"We all have," Lahr nodded, "an' there's men been double-crossed for a considerable sight less. An' on top of that—if he could get shucked of us—Kurt would have this whole spread plumb free an' beyond touchin'. It kinda makes a man think," the range boss said, slow and thoughtful. "There's a pile of good graze bein' held by this outfit. If he could cut loose of us—"

"But that's where we got him," Hennessy grinned, feeling better. "He can't chuck us out if we don't want t' go."

"Oh, can't he?" Lahr said, and spat contemptuously.

The cook sat still for a couple of heartbeats and then dark color moved into his cheeks. "All right—all right . . . I ain't *gone* yet! He might scare some of the dubs on this payroll but he sure couldn't bank on scarin' us *all* out."

"You talk like a fool! He could *sell* us out, couldn't he?"

The cook started swearing in a tight, bitter way.

Lahr lifted a knee, hooked a spur on the bench and sat there impassive with his green-eyed gaze still roving the hills. He waited till the cook had run through his rage, till the breath ran out of his wicked talk and his shoulders sagged back against the bunkhouse wall. Then he put his plan before Hennessy.

As he let it unfold the cook's mouth fell open and fear grew bright in his eyes for a moment and then faded away before the creep of desire. Lahr knew then he had this man and could use him; and he rammed home his points soft and swift and sat back.

"But what about the others? What about Krailor an' Shiloh Frayne?"

"Do you feel like you got to look out for them?"

"Well, no . . . I guess not," Hennessy said, with his thoughts still pawing it. "But will it work?" he asked worriedly, still a little afraid.

"It'll work if you remember what I said an' keep your mouth shut. I don't think you'll spill nothing. You an' me is the only ones in on this deal an' if anythin' leaks out I'll know what to do about it."

The cigar-smoking drummer in the yellow shoes and derby rode into St. David at ten o'clock of a star-sprinkled evening on a buttermilk filly that still looked to have a deal of miles left in her.

There was nothing spectacular about his arrival.

He passed up the first two or three darkened farms, turning finally down a lane to where a two-storied house still showed a lighted window. He hitched the filly to a post, brushed his clothes off a little, stepped up onto the veranda and put his knuckles to the door.

After a while he rapped again and presently a man with his hair every whichway and a pair of rough pants pulled on over his nightshirt came to the door with his galluses dangling.

He had a lamp in one hand and a pistol in the other.

"Yeah?" he said.

"Your name Scowsen?"

The lamp holder nodded.

"I'd like to have a fresh horse. My name's Sollantsy."

One further moment the man looked him over. "Barn's around to the back. I'll fetch out a lantern," he said, and closed the door.

Unhitching the filly, the man who called himself Sollantsy

led her on around back. Directly the man came out with his lantern and they crossed the yard to where a large red barn comfortably squatted in the shadows. The man hung his lantern on a peg inside the door and several horses nickered softly from a long row of stalls. There were six horses stabled there and none of them was work stock.

"That roan geldin' suit you?"

Sollantsy nodded and the man led him out. The derby-hatted drummer then walked over to the kak-pole and lifted down a forty-pound stock saddle, got himself a dry blanket and bridle and proceeded to get the roan ready for travel. He looked around at the man once. "I want that filly given extra good care."

The man had already taken the saddle and pad off. "Will you be wantin' any grub?" he grunted.

"No. But I'll be glad of fresh water."

"There's a spring-fed pipe just outside the door yonder."

"Which way to Benson?"

"About a half mile east you'll strike a north-south road. Turn left an' stay with it."

"How far?"

"Seven mile, more or less."

Sollantsy nodded. With an economy of movement he went up to the roan, pulled the slack from the latigo and swung up into the saddle. No money changed hands. "Take care of that filly," he said, and rode out.

An hour later he was dismounting at the Benson Livery.

Leaving his horse there he stepped up to an all-night lunch wagon, downed a couple sandwiches and a mug of hot java, scouted out a hotel and signed for a room. "Like some writin' materials," he told the yawning baldhead. "One envelope'll do."

The frowsty old clerk rummaged around and came up with the requested articles. "Hell of a time to be writin' a letter."

"You know how it is with a woman." Sollantsy winked.

The bald clerk grunted. "Only kinda woman I ever felt the need of is the kind that's near enough t' crawl into bed with. You don't hev t' write them no letters."

Sollantsy chuckled, picked up his things and went down a dim-lit hall hunting numbers.

Inside his room he turned the key in the lock, scratched a match and lit the lamp and set his writing things down on the wash stand. He tossed his coat on the bed. He set pitcher and washbasin carefully on the floor. He got a cigar from his vest and lighted it over the chimney of the lamp and pulled up a chair and sat down by the washstand.

He remained there a while, silently smoking and thinking. Then he yawned, squeezed the sweat off his forehead and let his breath go in a prolonged sigh. He got up again then, slipped his shoulder harness off and hung it on the back of his chair. Resuming his seat once more he picked up the pen and dipped it into the inkpot.

He wrote for an hour, filling four pages with cramped lines of words. Then he folded them into the envelope, sealed and addressed it and put on his coat and took it down to the clerk.

After which he went to bed.

11

MELODY IN LEAD

*T*HE STAGE STATION at Bisbee was no better and no worse than those she had found at half a hundred other towns, decided the girl now seated on the dusty and knife-scarred waiters' bench in the trapped heat beneath its sun-warped wooden awning. Dingy, faded and paintless, it looked to have plumped itself down against the face of a cliff in much the same fashion as some careless roustabout had plumped down the twelve sacks of grain that took up one end of the dust-windrowed planks beneath the bench on which she was seated.

The girl was dressed in dove-gray, tight-waisted taffeta with a ruffle of lace and black ribbon at her throat, the whole buffly powdered—like her hat and her gloves—with the dust from the road.

In the opinion of the man lounged against the sacked feed she was quite a looker. He'd been covertly observing her ever since he had stepped up here, though she hadn't thus far appeared to notice his presence.

Now he looked at her boldly. "Kinda tiresome waitin'," he offered conversationally. "Stage won't git in fer a hour yet."

"Thank you," she said, without turning her head.

"No trouble a-tall. Goin' t' Tucson?" he asked.

Again she nodded, still without turning.

Snooty, he decided.

But she sure was a looker. And the way that dress fit from the hips on up was enough to stop the U. S. Cavalry. If a feller could shine up to something like that, getting hitched wouldn't be half bad, he decided, and went over to the horse he had left at the porch edge.

Three riders on slow-moving horses were coming up the dusty road. Punchers, it looked like. He gave them no attention. Rummaging in the slicker lashed behind his cantle he dug out an apple. Been figuring to eat it himself but he reckoned he could get along without it. Polishing it briskly on a leg of his pants he moved back to the girl and held it out. "Mebbe you'd be likin' t' sink yer teeth in this?"

She looked at him then, and at the apple, also. "No, thank you." But she smiled the smallest bit and, encouraged, he said, "Long ride t' Tucson—be a good while 'fore you git there."

"Yes," she said, and looked away again.

He scowled at the apple, abruptly tossed it up and caught it. Then he wiped it again on his pantsleg and bit it. "Hev many hosses back East where you come from?"

"Quite a few."

"Good as this 'un?" He waved the apple he was chewing toward the horse he had left at the porch edge.

The three horsemen had come abreast of them and turned in at a hitchrack directly across from them. The three riders swung down and went into the building. Still chewing, Jupe Krailor said, "Good as him?"

"I'm afraid I don't know enough about horses to say."

"Don't eh?" He dragged a calloused hand across his scraggle of whiskers. "What you figgerin' t' go t' Tucson fer?"

"Well . . . really!" she said; and then suddenly she was smiling. "How many children do you have?"

"Huh! Who—*me?*" His cheeks took fire and he backed off a little. "Hell, I ain't even married—or about t' be!"

"That *is* queer, isn't it? You were taking such a fatherly interest—"

But the man was moving off. Catching up the grounded reins of his horse, with his neck still red he set off across the road.

That building over there was the Copper State Bank, easily the most pretentious looking edifice in town. The evening shadows, she noticed, were lengthening, that from the bank reaching almost to her feet. The long dusty street with its clutter of wagons and hitched horses showed but very few people; probably most of them were home getting their faces washed for supper.

A scurry of wind picked up dust from the roadway and, three doors down, a dog came off a porch and commenced to root beneath it. She could hear the hard beat of a blacksmith's hammer and a man's head and shoulders pushed through the batwings of the saloon next door and sent a speculative look in her direction, afterward withdrawing.

She looked for the man who had thought to be a ladykiller and found him over against the hitchrack where the three men had left their horses. Her glance considered him, idly noting his worn and grimed clothing, the battered hat which he wore, and she remembered the long uncombed hair curling down around his collar. Some range rider, probably, though he had more the look of a grubline rider, she thought, recalling his run-over boots and discolored spurs. She thought it odd how his appearance was so little in keeping with that of his horse, which was a good one suggesting plenty of bottom—like the horses beside which he stood now and whittled.

He seemed absorbed in his task, yet she had the impression

that his sharp little eyes were on her still; and she felt vaguely uncomfortable.

The sunlight was bright and golden where the blue-black shadows hadn't rubbed it out. Heat still clung to the underside of the station's warped wooden awning and she looked again at the horses, wondering about the three men in the bank, oddly surprised that they should have such good mounts. A roan, a bay and a white-stockinged sorrel. They looked a deal more like race horses than cowponies.

The station agent came with his slow limp to the doorway and poked his head out, giving her an encouraging smile. "It'll git here finally—allus does," he said. "Why don't you go over to the Rimrock House—that's the hotel yonder—where you'll be more comfortable. I'll see that you don't miss it—"

"If you don't mind, I'd rather wait here," she said.

"Lord, *I* don't mind!" He laughed a little at the vehemence of his words. And to make sure she properly understood him, he said, "We put that bench there for the convenience of our customers."

He couldn't figure her out. She'd come in with an escort of troopers from Camp Grant; the sergeant had confided that she'd had a bad scare. She didn't look scared; she was the coolest looking woman he had seen in a long while, and the most strikingly unusual. Blackest hair, whitest teeth and reddest lips he'd ever seen. But it was her eyes, he reckoned, that really got hold of you. Hazel. Clear and deep as mountain water. Honest. The most honest eyes he had ever encountered. He had never seen a woman quite like her, and the thought made him wish that he were twenty years younger and not chained down with a job at a stage depot.

He sighed and went back to his cluttered desk.

The girl turned her face and looked off down the road again. With its tortuous trails and cliff-flanked street she thought this was one of the ugliest towns she had ever been in. The raw red earth of the hillsides was the depressing color of rusted iron, and the houses she saw on the yonder slopes were little better or bigger than packing crates. How in the world did folks live in a place like this?

She pondered the question but what she had seen of it gave her no answer. She did not have to wonder what they did for amusement. The mines had fetched them here in the first place, of course, and what wealth they wrenched from the stubborn earth went mostly into the saloons and brothels, of which there were plenty.

The old, old story of the wild frontier.

She frowned a little, considering it. How could better things come where men lived hardly more civilized than animals, where toil and greed and savagery were the common order of the day? Was all life harsh? Was there nowhere anything better than this? What of love and warmth and graciousness—were these nothing but words on a printed page?

She shook loose of her thoughts with an impatient lift of her shoulders. Love and graciousness, like freedom, were all very well, but the first need in life was security. She was not a bargaining woman, but security was something she never had known. It was the most desirable thing she could think of.

The mood was abruptly shattered, her eyes drawn sharply across the street by the sound of a muffled explosion. Over there, by the hitchrack, the would-be ladykiller had dropped his whittling and now, to her surprise, he had a rifle cradled in his arms and the reins of four horses were in his left hand.

Two men with heavy sacks were backing out of the bank; a third, back toward her, still stood in the doorway with a gun in his fist, his face obscured behind the folds of a pulled-up neckerchief. And the two with the sacks were masked likewise, she saw, as they coolly turned and stepped across to their horses.

She heard boots sound behind her and the agent's grim voice. "Inside, miss—quick!" And then he was brushing past her, a determined man with a shotgun. Crouching low, he dived for the pile of sacked feed but, just short of it, he stopped and straightened. With a tight, choked cry he suddenly buckled in his tracks, his dropped gun clattering across the warped planks.

Smoke drifted whitely from the ladykiller's rifle. Gun sound clouted the fronts of the buildings and, even as she watched, the man whirled and with another burst of firing drove three punchers behind the Lone Star Cafe.

The men with the sacks were mounted now, fighting their rearing horses. And then they were gone, dust billowing behind them as they cut for the open range.

The man in the Copper State's doorway chose that moment to whirl and come pelting toward the hitchrack where the other man waited with the two remaining horses. The lady-killer tossed him the reins of one of them, swung onto his own and drove a final shot toward the Lone Star Cafe. He was wheeling his horse to take after the others when a man came onto a porch two doors down. The slanting shafts of the sun kicked light from his lifting rifle, from the bit of metal that was pinned to his vest.

Flame knifed brightly from the crouched-forward shape of the man still afoot, and the girl saw the lawman stagger against the wall. But the man who had shot him wasn't satisfied. Again flame spurted from the muzzle of his gun and the lawman folded across the porch rail.

He sheathed his pistol then and jerked his horse's head around and hauled himself into the saddle. "Come on—come on!" his companion shouted; and they churned up the dust in a great wide circle. As they swept past the stage office the man who had shot the badge-toter suddenly lifted a hand as though to clutch at his hat. If that was his intention it got there too late, for the hat sailed off and he did not stop for it but spurred after his companion with his red hair flying wild in the wind.

12

AN OLD TROLLOP EXPLODES

THE COLONEL was very sorry Kurt had had this trip for nothing but Miss Balinett, he said, was no longer around. Yes, the troopers had intercepted the stage robbers and had fetched her in unharmed, but she'd been in a swivvet to get to Tucson and had gone with an escort to catch the stage at Bisbee.

The nizzy old gaffer had wanted to discuss horses but Kurt had cut the talk short, bribed a tarp from the sutler's wife and, sprawled still dressed across it, had slept the clock very nearly around.

That had been three days ago. Refreshed, shaved and washed in the creek, he had quit Camp Grant early yesterday morning and had made good time, considering the amount of traveling Snuffy had done in the past five days.

He knew there'd be no use in him going to Bisbee; long before he could get there the girl would be gone. So he'd struck straight for Tucson, cutting across the country by the shortest means available; and now he could see it, just yonder—a scattering of light beneath the black shadows of the Santa Catalinas.

He held the big dun to a leisurely lope despite the impatience that prodded him. This conservation of horseflesh was an old thing with Cardigan who never knew when he might really need every ounce of speed he could get. Sometimes he would ride for hours at a walk, and had done so on this trip, for in a country life this—and in his kind of business —another ten yards of travel might spell all the difference between continued living and an unmarked grave.

Sometimes, like now, when his mind got to thinking of the risks he ran and the mighty little pleasure he got out of the business, he wondered if horse stealing ever really paid. He knew, of course, it was the soft streak in him that turned his mind along such daunsy trails. But a man couldn't keep from thinking.

It was numbskulls, mostly, that played the outlaw game; puny little bastards, too weak for honest living, and the lazy lads that would go to any length to keep from turning their hands at any regular job. These, and the natural born bullies and chiselers, made up the bulk of the owlhoot legions. The exceptions were plain damn fools like himself who had a craving for excitement and didn't have the gumption to keep a rein on it.

Sometimes, he thought, he'd give anything to be honest, to get his damn feet back on the straight and narrow. But the same old thought always struck him each time he figured to sponge the slate clean and start over. Just one more haul . . . just one more haul and he'd quit the damn game. But it was ever and always the same old story. Like drinking hard likker, riding the owlhoot got to be a habit; and he knew in his bones there was just one end to it.

But one of these days he *would* quit—he *really* would. Maybe if this girl was his kind, if she was something to be proud of, he might even start over for her sake.

He laughed a little, wryly, at the foolishness of any such notion as that. He might quit, but it wouldn't be on account of no skirt.

The game wasn't what it had used to be. Times were changing. The country was getting too damned settled up. The risks were greater and the profits much leaner—it was a dog's life at best and, with the cattlemen organizing like they was all over, it was getting, by cripes, so you couldn't turn around without ramming into some kind of star-packer.

He thought about that for the next couple miles. And he thought of the dude and Frank Esparza and the loose-jawed way of that liveryman, Reagan. He kept seeing the dude and Esparza eyeing Snuffy. . . .

The writing was on the wall, all right. It might be a good thing for him to quit right now—to get out of this business and live like a Christian. The boys might not much cotton to it, but a bigger share in the pot they'd built up ought to wipe the scowls off their faces. Last winter had sweetened the kitty plenty—they must have pretty near twenty thousand right now. Split five ways that wouldn't be too bad. If he were to add from his own another five hundred to each man's share . . .

It was sure as hell worth considering, he thought; and then he called himself seven kinds of a fool for even dreaming up such a cockeyed notion. He must, by Gawd, be going soft in the head!

But the notion stayed with him all the way down the slope to the Santa Cruz Valley.

He'd been lucky, up to now; but no man's luck continued good forever, and all the signs and signal smokes gave urgent warning his was headed for the rocks. There was that dude and Esparza and what this chase had shown him about that bastard Grave Creek Clanton! That was gratitude for you!

They were all alike, this ragtag breed of the chaparral. All cut from the same rotten cloth! Shifty, greedy, an untrustworthy lot whose allegiance was worth no more than the size of the cut it got them. And when that cut seemed no longer sufficient—or other interests provided a chance that looked better—they would sell you out to the quickest bidder.

It was a time to be thinking, to be adding the score up. And he did so.

Something was plain enough to Cardigan then. He'd better pay off his crew and get them out of the country—give 'em the whole damn pot if he had to. But get rid of them. Now. Before it was too late.

He came into Tucson by a woodchopper's trail, still moodily thinking as he followed it through the squalid Mexican quarter, and so into the brighter lights of Meyer Street. There was a stage pulled up before the Overland office and the sight pulled his mind back around to Docie.

He ground-tied the dun and stepped into the office. A Mexican at the counter was buying a ticket for Yuma. Kurt looked at the clerk; this wasn't the fellow he had accosted when he'd come here to meet the woman from St. Louis—Cripes, but that seemed a long time ago! This was a bull-necked guy with pink sleeve garters. A pair of iron-rimmed spectacles sat on his nose and he gave Kurt a look over the tops of them. Counting out the Mexican's change he said: "Well?"

"Was you round when today's stage got in from Bisbee?"

"Yup."

Kurt was having a little trouble with his swallower. "I was supposed t' meet a woman—"

"Wasn't no woman on it."

Kurt frowned. "I don't reckon you could be mistaken?"

"I don't make mistakes," the agent said testily. "There was jest three people got offa that stage. Breckenridge, Fowler an' a lady—there wasn't no woman on it."

One of Cardigan's big fingers traced a brand some puncher had carved in the counter. "Lady, eh? What kinda lookin' lady?"

"Best damn looker that ever hit *this* burg. Class—real class. You ever see Lizette—that one they called the 'Flying Nymph' that was here with the Monarch crowd last year? She couldn't hold a candle to this one."

"Pretty well stacked up, eh?"

"Like a basket of chips."

"You didn't catch her name?"

"Come off it, pal. She didn't look like nothin' you'd be figurin' to meet."

Outside, with Snuffy's reins in his hand, Cardigan stood a while, thoughtful. He guessed it probably wasn't her, but it could be. That bull-necked ox in the stage office might call any skirt a lady that wasn't over forty and his ideas of feminine pulchritude might not gee at all with the facts of the business. Still, he ought to make sure. If it happened to be Docie and she really was a looker, he'd be a fool to go off and . . .

With a curse he swung into the saddle. How the hell did you go about finding a woman when you didn't even know what she looked like?

He didn't realize he'd spoken the thought aloud till a kid, peering up at him, said with a grin, "You might try the hotels."

Of course! That was it! The hotels, if she'd put up at one of them, would have her name on the register.

He tossed the kid a cartwheel and turned Snuffy's head toward the Empire House which was not over six doors away up the street.

But she wasn't there, and she wasn't at any other of the places he tried. There was no Balinett on their books that he could find.

To hell with her then. He had spent enough time traipsin round on her account. He'd step into Long Tooth Emma's here and scour the trail dust from his gullet. If Docie wanted to find him she could come out to the ranch.

Long Tooth Emma's was the same inside as he'd remembered it. Biggers, the banker, was over at the bar shooting the breeze with three or four ranchers and Emma, togged out in her silks and satins, was fanning herself in the horsehair rocker.

"Well!" she said with a grin when she saw him, and bounced up out of her chair and came over. "You've certainly set *this* town on its ear!"

"Me?" Kurt looked at her blankly.

"You!" She grinned, and gave him a playful push with her hand. "Stella Mae'll have something to say to you—cryin' her eyes out ever since she heard it. Putting on the dog, aren't you, Cardigan?"

He looked at her, frowning. Under this banter there was a hard core of something he couldn't quite nail; and he didn't get that stuff about Stella Mae, either. What the hell did *she* have to cry about?

He cuffed back his hat. "Come off it," he said. "I come in for a drink—"

"You mean you're not serving liquor?"

Cardigan wheeled his shoulders half around, and stopped. "I don't get it."

Miss Emma bared her golden fangs. "Now listen, dearie. I always say 'live and let live.' How you latch onto your money ain't nobody's business but your own, I say. But after all"— the coy smile showed a tight streak of malice—"you don't find me antigodlin around trying to get myself in the horse business, do you?"

She was riled, all right, no doubt about that. But he still couldn't think why she'd be on the prod with him. And he was too damn tired to care one way or the other. She was right about one thing. How he got his money was no business of hers.

He said: "If I ain't welcome in this dive—"

But she cut him off with a wave of her hands. "I got competition enough in this town without you importin' anything from outside—"

"What the hell are you talkin' about?"

"That stylish bitch you shipped in from Bisbee!"

A great light broke over Kurt. His eyes opened wide and then closed to slits. "Where'd you get that stuff?"

"Don't give me that. It's all over town how she went into that stage office askin' for you!"

Beads of sweat stood out on Cardigan's forehead. "Why, you lyin' old—"

"It's you and this Balinett baggage we're discussing. Top Hat Charlie was right there when the stage come. He knew her, too. 'Docie Balinett!' he says." With a simpering smile she mimicked the Englishman's old-world preciseness.

Her green eyes spat flame.

Black rage looked out of Cardigan's stare. One big hand reached out and took her by the throat. The old harridan's voice flew into high C. Cardigan said with an oath: "She's not what you think—"

"D'you think I'm a *fool!* He knew her, I tell you—what's more, he hired a rig to drive her out to your place! You can't do this to me, Kurt Cardigan! You stick to your horses or I'll—"

Night's shadows, huge and monstrous, lay across the land. Smell of dust and sun-parched vegetation came windborne off the desert which stretched to the south like a dead dun sea. That wind waved the dry browning fronds of the pepper tree whose filmy branches laced the deeper dark piled up at the left of Miss Emma's parlor house, hiding the hitchracks and the customers' horses.

The stores and shops had closed long since so that most of this section of the street lay dark, though a thousand lights winked and gleamed and fluttered in the next block north where Honkytonk Row set the pace by which men lived and died, by which they fought and had their hopes and guarded secrets—Honkytonk Row with its raucous many-tongued voice ever calling the unwary with its siren song and tawdry show of a joy it never fulfilled.

Flinging out of the harlots' house, Cardigan half turned that way in the natural impulse of a man hard used. But the clank of his spurs suddenly stilled and he stood there, caught in the churn of his tumultuous thoughts. Drink might warm the cold pit of his belly, but it would not mend the mistakes he had made or make black white no matter how much of the stuff he poured down.

For man cannot alter the things he has done. He may hide them away but their taste remains with him. Smart though he be, and wondrous conniving, he cannot turn back the cold hands of time. The finger writes, but neither piety nor wit can lure it back to cancel half a line.

Who first put that truth on paper was possessed of a wisdom dearly learned, Kurt thought with a bitter scowl. For he had found it true, and that knowledge was a fire burning through him now—a lifted axe about to sever the stay ropes of his life.

He had played the fool and here, too late, he knew it.

He must get to the ranch and get shed of his crew, get them off the place and out of the country. It did not occur to him they might demur at any such precipitate departure, or that it might be more practical to depart himself. They were men with a price, every one of them; pay that price and they did your bidding—the belief was founded on past experience. And he was not himself concerned with flight, but only with covering the tracks of past errors.

A more discerning man would have found irony in the thought that a painted old trollop like Long Tooth Emma should finally have brought Kurt face to face with himself and a solid realization that crime did not pay. The finer nuances of the scene he had just been through were lost on Kurt; he was occupied solely with the most obvious aspect of what he had heard—that the wolf-fanged old slut of a parlorhouse madam should imagine he was importing high-priced hookers because a looker who had asked for him happened to be acquainted with a lunger whose living came from pounding out tunes on a flophouse piano!

It was enough to make a guy heave up his breakfast. But the part that got Kurt was them *knowing* each other! And her from St. Louis!

With an oath he plunged into the loamy blackness that concealed the racks and hitched horses. He knew pretty well where he had left the dun but it was so goddam black you couldn't hardly see your own hand before your face.

Then he remembered he'd trained Snuffy to come at his whistle. He gave him a call and the dun stallion nickered. Further over to the left and back a little.

Kurt moved toward the sound, thinking what a hell of a trap this would make if some fellow who had it in for him happened to know about him leaving old Snuffy out here. Be a natural for him. When Kurt opened his mouth to call out to the horse, all the guy would have to do would be to haul out his gun and start triggering.

A sweat came out round Kurt's collar and he stopped and stood listening. He couldn't hear anything but the restless stomp of some hitched pony's hoofs but something told him not to whistle again.

He was in a fever of impatience to be out of this town, to begin that respectable Christian life he envisioned for himself so soon as he could separate from past activities and present personnel. As is generally the way with reforming characters, old associations were become abhorrent to him; he was in a lather to remove himself from all corroding influences.

But he was not in such a sweat he meant to risk being tagged by any powder-sped blue whistler. There were times when speed was best made slowly, when the better part of valor had nothing to do with poking your chin out.

He moved with extreme caution, eyes raking the shadows, feet testing out the ground before he put his weight on them. This was plain horse sense, a part of the pattern by which his kind were enabled to continue a precarious existence. The graveyards were filled with damn fools who'd got careless and he was more than half convinced that, somewhere in this devil's brew of blackness, some belly-crawling sidewinder was waiting to pot him.

He spent a long ten minutes scouting out the dun's position, afterwards swearing in a relieved kind of anger when it became at last apparent he had the place to himself.

He tightened the cinch and stepped into the saddle.

By God, it would be *good* to get out of this business. Another couple days and he'd be shooting at his shadow!

He let out a tired breath and kneed Snuffy toward the street.

It was just as he reached it, where the light fell full on him, that a figure stepped out of the harness shop doorway.

"I'd like a little talk with you."

13

"DO YOU RECOGNIZE THIS PICTURE?"

CARDIGAN stopped, turned completely still.

Cold sweat came out on the backs of his hands and a risen wind, clouting in off the desert, lifted a spiral of dust from the street and sent it spinning off into the darkness.

A flat moment of silence followed. Then Esparza's voice said: "Do much ridin' at night?"

A look of smoldering violence brightened Cardigan's stare but he fought down the urge of his roaring blood. "You stop me to find that out?"

"Just wondered. Been out to your place at night twice kinda recent. Seemed funny not findin' nobody home. You been losin' any horses?"

Cardigan considered. "Not that I know of. Hard t' tell without checkin'."

"Thought mebbe your boys was out watchin' for horse thieves."

Cardigan looked at him then, quick and quiet, thin of lip. "If you come out to buy horses why'd you come at night?"

"Came the first time one mornin'. No one home but your cook."

A kind of stillness settled.

"Well?" said Kurt sharply.

Esparza shrugged. He lifted his pipe stem and rubbed at his chin with it. "Lot of ranchers been losin' horses round here. Too many. They don't like it. As a breeder yourself you can understand their feelin's."

Cardigan nodded. "Stealin' horses," he said, "is a bad line of work for a man to be in."

"Yes," Esparza said, "a very chancy business. When a horse thief's caught, more often than not he's found with his neck stretched, danglin' from a tree limb. You ever think about that?"

Cardigan sat very still in the saddle, with his head slightly tipped, looking down at the man. He searched the marshal's face with a hard, steady probing.

But there was nothing to be read from Esparza's wrinkled features. Neither friendliness nor hostility. The pale surface of his eyes looked back at Cardigan unwinking.

The big rancher's control was beginning to wear thin. Bright flecks, like wildness, danced through his stare and the refracted light from the yonder saloons showed a glistening of sweat along the curves of his cheeks. But in the end some tag-end of caution made him softly say: "Why should I?"

Esparza made a gesture with his pipe stem. "Want to tell you a story, Cardigan. Chances are it won't much interest you, but I'd like you to hear it anyway. It concerns a young feller of about your age who come into this country several years

ago. We didn't have much law around here at that time but
there was plenty of room an' plenty opportunities for a man
that didn't mind takin' a little chance."

Esparza tapped the dottle from his pipe, rummaged round
in his pockets and brought up fresh tobacco. "This feller could
of made him a stake at most anythin' he felt like turnin' his
hand to; he was smart an' likable, had some wheels in his
think-box. He took a whack at minin', tried some freightin', a
little ranchin'. Could of done all right at any of 'em, but the
work was hard an' the money come a little too slow for his
likin'."

He looked up and studied Cardigan a moment. He finished
packing his pipe and put the tobacco away. "This feller had a
broad streak of recklessness in him. Patience wasn't one of his
virtues. He looked around, sized up the layout, saw what
other men were doin'. Some of those gents were skatin' on the
thin edge of turnin' into what Judge Honnifer describes as
'undesirable citizens.' "

Cardigan's shape did not relax in the saddle. His lips made
a solid, bitter roll across his face and his eyes were bleakly ex-
pressionless, watchful.

Esparza said, "Our friend was no crook. He didn't aim to
become one, but that reckless streak in him was beginnin' to
turn yeasty. Men were maverickin' cattle an' gettin' big at it;
gamblers were livin' off the fat of the land. Our friend saw no
reason why he shouldn't take a little fling at quicker profits
himself.

"Up north in Colorado, in Wyomin' an' Montana where the
grass was good and the ranches far apart, there was a lot of
good horseflesh driftin' round without brands. Yearlin's an'
two-year-olds—some aged stuff, too. Horses was cheap in that
country but down here they would fetch a good price. If you
had them.

"Originally, he prob'ly figured on payin' for 'em, but there
was this brash streak in him. All he really needed was an or-
ganization an' there was plenty of young sports, brash as himself, that would jump at the chance once they knew what the
plan was."

Esparza dug out a match and looked up at Kurt slanchways. "This stuff borin' you?"

"Go on," breathed Cardigan.

"Well, this guy started to work an' made a pretty good thing of it. Got his horses up there an' sold 'em down here. Prob'ly had a few hideouts along the way, relay stations with other gents workin' 'em. Lot of ranchers'll rest horses if you can show 'em a profit in it. This feller was smart. Worked the business two years without crowdin' his luck. Built up quite a spread in this country, an' a name for horses of the very top quality—stock with run in it an' plenty of bottom.

"Then the picture changed. Those fellers up north got hep to themselves. Small colt crops an' too much shrinkage in their usin' stock made them start to look around. They put some men on the job an' caught an' swung a few fellers but our friend slipped through them; he was still in the clear, tracks covered. He'd enough stock on hand that he could be what people thought him an' become an honest breeder."

Cardigan sat there, neither speaking nor moving while fiddle scrape and the clink of glasses mixed with drunken shouts and laughter became loud sounds in the increasing quiet that stretched between himself and Esparza.

Time stood still.

Impatience lifted Cardigan's shoulders.

The marshal sighed and scratched his match. Smoke came out of his mouth round the pipe stem.

"Here was a feller growin' up with the country, gettin' his start like too many others; still, I'm bound to admit, no worse than buildin' up a spread with one cow an' a runnin' iron. He wasn't takin' no bread from the widders an' orphans. When them northern boys clamped down on his game it left him two choices—he could quit an' go straight or he could shift his operations to some other locality.

"I'd like to tell you he quit, an' he may have done so. He commenced sellin' mounts to the cavalry an' nobody kicked there was anything wrong with it. But a man don't readily pass up an easy profit—or shake loose of a bunch he has et, stole an' slept with. It was hard to believe his whole crowd had gone straight or that he'd got rid of them an' had a new honest crew. Once a man goes in for that kind of thing it's a pretty tough business tryin' to feel content with the smaller profits an' hateful routine of square livin'.

"Times had changed. Law of a sort had come into this country. Its enforcement was bound to change things still more, cramping down a man's freedom, puttin' a fence around initiative. It was not a harsh law or an avengeful one; but it was there all the same. Although plainly inclined to let sleepin' dogs lay, this law—with its rigid set of rules an' forbiddin's —must have represented to a man grown used to doin' as he pleased an intolerable restraint, a constant challenge and irritation.

"Do you follow me?"

The glitter of sweat was on Cardigan's forehead. "You talk," he said, "like that Camp Pickett preacher."

"A sharp man," the marshal nodded. "I wish our friend might have known him better. Might of been the means of improvin' his outlook. Of mebbe keepin' his feet on the straight and narrer."

He sucked at his pipe in a thoughtful silence. "I want you to see the Law's position. If this feller had quit he was entitled to a break. We had no proof he hadn't quit. But about three months ago, more or less, a bunch of ranchers usin' land in the north end of this Territory started howlin' they was losin' horses—not culls or colts but top usin' horses, the cream of their remudas.

"They carried their complaints to the Governor. All sheriffs an' marshals was warned, descriptions of some of the horses sent out—cattlemen's associations alerted. Maybe our friend wasn't aware of this; he got to doin' a lot of night ridin', keepin' out of sight in the daytime. The word got around. Nothin' definite, of course, just loose straws in the wind, little drawin's apart, a look in folks' eyes when his name was mentioned."

The silence closed in and got deeper and deeper till it shut out completely all sound from up yonder. The run of Cardigan's breathing became audible.

"You—you think this guy was doin' it?"

Esparza shrugged. "Somebody was—and still is. Forty head of horses was lifted two weeks ago from the neighborhood of Chandler. Bunch of mares an' colts were run off a couple nights later from a ranch in Oak Creek Canyon; then this bunch hit Amado, then Cortaro, then Florence."

A wildness lay in Cardigan's eyes.

"This same bunch?"

Esparza said: "There's a pattern to these things that a man can't escape. A thief starts small but the habit grows on him. Violence breeds violence. The man who'll snatch a purse today will be in the mood to rob a bank tomorrow. Do you recognize the picture?"

14

THE TASTE OF DEATH

CARDIGAN'S laugh was short and ugly. "I don't think your man will rob any banks."

Esparza considered him and then looked at his horse. He had his own private thoughts but no reflection of these was permitted to alter the planes of his face. Yet his glance, when he finally lifted it, held the look of a man who has lived too long on the edge of violence, who has gone too long with the run of the pattern.

"I do not think your opinion or mine will much help him. He, or the men he thinks for, have turned their backs on caution. The bank at Douglas was gutted two nights ago. A stage south of Tombstone was stuck up yesterday morning. In broad daylight yesterday evening the same pack of wolves robbed the Copper State Bank at Bisbee."

"If you're suggestin'—"

The marshal held up his hand. "You can be hung just as high for a sheep as a goat and humans, generally speaking, like horses, are mostly judged on past performance." He regarded Cardigan quietly. "If you should happen to bump into him, tell this man he's through. There is just one thing that might possibly straighten him out—complete restitution and the prompt apprehension of every man connected with what happened at Bisbee yesterday."

Docie Balinett, seated on the leather covered springs of the buggy seat alongside the consumptive Britisher, thought she had never seen anything quite like this country in all her twenty-two years. The vastness of it was immeasurable and the effect both majestic and terrifying. Rugged mountains, great upthrust slabs of barren rock by their look, hemmed it in with barbaric shades of blue and purple, a burning waste of sand, silence and desolation.

"But what do people find to do out here?"

Top Hat Charlie's rheumy eyes showed a twinkle. "Ranching, mining and hell-raising, mostly. I say, it's not really bad once you're used to it. Some fine chaps out here—quite heroic, really. Take this fellow, Cardigan."

"Yes?" Docie prompted.

Charlie looked at the back of the horse a few moments. They had already covered the past pretty thoroughly, the people they'd known, the places they'd been—Abilene, Dodge City, Cheyenne, Deadwood, Virginia City, Brady, San Saba, Coffeeville and a hundred other places a shade less hectic in between. Neither had dwelt at much length on current affairs. "I make out to keep on eating," the Britisher offered with a little smile. And Docie explained, "I haven't met this man Cardigan—yet."

Charlie's look, when she'd mentioned that, had seemed a little queer; and it was queer again now, Docie thought, regarding his profile. Not a look you could take apart and label. More a kind of withdrawing; a tightening of the mouth, a general air of reticence—as though his eyes were windows, she thought, and someone had drawn the blinds.

She said, "Heroic? I thought he was a rancher."

"I guess he is, after a fashion. Has a place just south of Oracle—sells horses to the cavalry. Don't know much about him, really. Keeps himself to himself, if you know what I mean. We don't see him much down around Tucson."

"But why call him 'heroic'?"

Charlie studied the horse's tail. "Perhaps," he said, " 're-markable' would be a more apt description," and lapsed off into silence.

For a time, as the buggy creaked and groaned toward the hills, Docie gave her attention to the country about her, to considering the thorny bushes and different kinds of cactus. Charlie clucked to the horse and made occasional small talk, commenting on flora and fauna, the condition of the range, weather prospects and mineral deposits.

But at last Docie seemed to have had enough of it. She said: "Charlie, I want to know more about Cardigan."

He flicked a fly off the horse's flank with a shake of the lines. "What do you want to know about him?"

"I want to know why you looked funny when I mentioned him."

"Did I?"

"And why you called him remarkable."

Charlie said, reflectively: "Wouldn't you call a man re-markable who showed up in a place about three years ago with nothing but a horse and the clothes on his back and is now generally regarded as the greatest horse breeder in that section of country?"

"Well . . . yes," she nodded, "I guess perhaps I should. But that doesn't account for the way you looked, does it?"

He didn't immediately answer. Instead his eyes came around and considered her. There was speculation in his look, a little embarrassment also. "Must we talk about him?"

"I'd rather." She said soberly, "You've either said too much or not enough, Charlie."

He studied the lines in his hands for a moment. Then he lifted his eyes and looked straight ahead. "It's absolutely none of my business, Docie, but I can't help wondering what in-terest you'd be having in common with Cardigan. He's— Well, to put the thing politely, he's a pretty tough character."

"Don't be stuffy. Say what you mean."

"You can't pin the man down that way. I could tell you he's a ruffian but that wouldn't give you the picture. Half the people in this country would fit that description."

"In what way is he different from the rest of the ruffians?"

"Well, he's no bully. He don't go around picking fights, yet he's not the kind of a man you'd want to cross."

"Why not?"

"I can't tell you that. I am not at all certain I know the answer myself. He's a hard man to know."

"You mean deep?"

His hand described an irritable gesture. "I don't know what I mean. The man's an enigma—you could question a dozen people and get as many different answers. He looks like a brush popper and talks like one. Most of the time he acts like one, too, but he's a long way from being just another dumb bruiser. When Cardigan speaks men listen."

"Quite a character," Docie smiled.

"He's more than a 'character,'" Top Hat Charlie said darkly. "He's a very dangerous man, my girl, and I'd advise you to keep away from him."

Docie's hazel eyes twinkled. "Have you not ever noticed what a compelling attraction a dangerous man has for a woman?"

He met her smile with a strange severity.

He drew a troubled breath and his glance searched her features with a sustained and dark conviction. "You're a mighty beautiful woman, Docie, but you're not the girl I knew in San Saba."

Docie lowered her eyes. Color passed through her cheeks. "You're bound to leave a few things behind when you set your foot on the rung of a ladder."

"You were very determined," he remembered. "You were going to be someone—"

"Yes," she said quickly, "but values change. As a person climbs he finds the view widening. I have discovered that a fence creates an optical illusion; it does not change the quality of the grass on either side."

He shook his head. He said regretfully, "I am afraid Abilene and Dodge City were not good for you."

She patted his knee. "Let's put that song away, Charlie. I've found it doesn't pay to look back. We all strike our bargains sooner or later; I've struck mine and I'm going through with it. Now tell me about yourself."

Charlie shrugged that away. "What are you doing in Tucson?"

"I came out here to marry a man," Docie said. "I came out here to marry Kurt Cardigan."

Charlie almost stopped the buggy in his shock. He looked at her with an expression of incredulity. "Are you crazy?"

Her eyes met his straightly. "What's so crazy about marrying a rancher?"

"But . . . Cardigan!"

He was plainly disturbed. It was in the quick lift of his chin, in what she saw staring at her out of his eyes.

She said, "Have you never been disgusted with the life you are living—with everything it stands for and all its surroundings? Two months ago in St. Louis I made up my mind that I had all I could take of it. A fresh start was what I wanted; a man to take care of me, a feeling of security. I put an ad in a paper offering to marry a rancher and Cardigan answered."

"You can't do it." His voice said bitterly: "I won't let you."

"It's not your concern."

"We'll see about that! Half this country thinks the man's a damn horse thief—do you think I will let you get mixed up with that?"

"I have made my bargain," Docie said, "and I will keep it."

Cardigan was two hours out of Tucson before he could do any coherent thinking and he was almost to Rickven's cabin before the marshal's words began to make any sense and uncover the picture in its proper perspective.

Anger ran through him like the feel of hot iron. Someone in his outfit had turned wolf and doublecrossed him. But the damage was done now and he was caught in the toils of it—caught like an ant in flypaper.

He had reached this point in his thinking when the nester's shack loomed up before him, a deeper black against the low-riding stars.

A cold wind flapped and fluttered in the trees, damp with the smell of the yonder pool. He had no illusions about Esparza's reasons in tipping his hand, about the marshal's purpose in showing a horse thief just where he stood.

Frank Esparza was smart, a great deal smarter than Cardigan had figured him. He knew his own limitations. He knew how far he would get fetching a badge-packing posse onto Cardigan's land. He knew he'd either find nothing and give the show clear away or he'd catch them with the goods and get a lot of men killed.

He never had much cottoned to gunplay and killing; it was one of the things folks liked him for. He never dragged a gun if he could manage to get around it. Handing Cardigan that line had got him round it very neatly. He'd shown Cardigan where he stood without presenting any occasion for gunplay. By the terms of his strategy if powder was burned it would be burned in the hills among a pack of wrangling chaparral wolves.

He'd put the whole business right square up to Cardigan. He hadn't mentioned Cardigan's name at all, but anyone would know he had been talking about Cardigan. Of course he'd made it appear like he didn't suppose Cardigan connected with this recent stuff, but he'd made it clear enough whose men he figured was doing it—and it was Cardigan he proposed to make responsible for their actions. Which was all fair enough if those banks and that stage had been stuck up by the KC crew.

But what if they hadn't?

Supposing Esparza was just guessing—was just presuming, because he'd pegged the KC crowd for a bunch of crooks, that it was Cardigan's men that had pulled those raids at Chandler, Amado, Cortaro and Florence?

He scrubbed a damp hand across bristly jowls. If the KC crew *had* pulled those raids it was quite in the cards they'd robbed the banks and stage also; but if the marshal had proof would he have wrapped the deal up in this kind of a package? Wouldn't it have been a heap more natural for him to have put Kurt Cardigan under arrest?

There was the crux of all Cardigan's thinking. Did the marshal have proof or didn't he? He could maybe have got on to what had happened up north but if he had any proof to what had happened around here—any proof he could give to a jury—why in hell would he be asking someone else to rake the chestnuts?

That wasn't the way a marshal worked in Cardigan's experience.

The smell of this night was strong in Kurt's nostrils as he sat idle in the leather trying to think his way through this. One thing was clear and one only. Regardless of how much or how little Esparza knew or suspected, the play left Cardigan right out in the open. He either played the cards Frank Esparza had dealt him or he became in full fact an out-and-out outlaw. No other interpretation could be put on the marshal's words.

He got out the makings and twisted up a smoke. Still absorbed in his thinking he was about to scratch a match when a voice said:

"Cardigan?"

Cardigan stiffened.

The voice said hurriedly: "It's me—Rickven. Over here by the door."

Cardigan said, half angry, "You pick a damn funny time to call out to a man."

"I'm not myself, I'm that worried. It's Lula—if you kin spare a couple minutes I sure wisht you would look at her."

"What's the matter with her?"

"She keeps moanin' an' groanin'—"

"I don't hear no moanin'," Cardigan said, but he got out of the saddle and followed the nester into his shack.

Rickven lighted a lamp. He was an ineffectual man, hollow chested and meaching, with a ten days' growth of whiskers on his face. "I tried t' hail thet other feller down, but . . ."

Cardigan brushed past him, his eyes going at once to the

red headed girl he had seen by the waterfall. He was shocked by the change in her appearance.

She was on a bunk in the corner with a shift twisted round her. Her red hair didn't look as though it had seen a comb in weeks and the lovely face he'd remembered was twisted and drawn, unnaturally flushed as with fever. The staring eyes didn't know him.

"Hell's fire!" he said, turning. "You can see what's ailin' her! What the hell you been thinkin' of? This ain't no place for a woman in her condition!"

Rickven's hangdog look slid away and came back again, sly and emboldened. "Who got her this way?"

Cardigan caught him by the shirtfront in a twisting grip. "You don't need t' look at me—an' you can wipe that damn smug look off your face! You know the kinda guys I got on my payroll—why the hell didn't you keep your eye on her?"

He flung him back against the wall. Going over to the bed he stood there scowling down at Lula.

"You're a hell of a father," he said, coming back. "Her time's about here. Ain't there some woman you could get t'—"

"What woman?" Rickven whined. "What woman would come up here, an' what would I be payin' her with if she did come?"

Cardigan pulled a roll of bills from his pocket and tossed them on the table. He saw the gleam that came into the nester's eyes, and said sharply: "That's for her—understand? It ain't t' buy you no whiskey with. You get a pill-roller out here an' do whatever he tells you t' do."

He started to go out and then paused with his hand on the door, looking back again, looking at Rickven carefully.

He said, "If you was a sheriff an' had got the deadwood on a bunch of damn rustlers, what would you do?"

A kind of sweat came out on the nester's cheeks.

"Say you caught the big dog right in town, had the drop on him. Would you spin him a story an' tip your hand or would you throw 'im in the jug?"

"I . . . I'd throw him in the jug."

Cardigan nodded. He didn't seem to notice the man had

licked his lips twice before any words came. Or that his cheeks had gone a dirty gray as Cardigan had spoken.

He went out and climbed into the saddle and turned Snuffy's nose in the direction of the ranch.

The moon was up now, a silver disc above the blue-black slopes of the mountain. Its argent light spilled across the range in a flood of ghostly radiance, lending commonplace things a majesty they seldom attained in daylight.

But Cardigan's mind was not concerned with beauty. He was listening again to the nester's words and nodding his head to the wisdom of them. It is easy to believe where one's own convictions are handed back in another man's voice.

Esparza had no proof. He'd been pulling a bluff in the hope Kurt Cardigan would do his work for him. A pretty sharp biscuit—and he'd come mighty near putting it over. Not that Kurt would have turned his own crew over to the law, but . . . Even now Kurt grimaced when he thought how near he'd come to playing the fool. He must be losing his grip or going soft in the head. The KC crew must be sharing that thought to go out on their own and be sticking up banks and stagecoaches! By God—

He tipped his shape in the saddle to fling a quick look at the black piled-up shadows of that brush on his left and was like that, turning, when something like a gigantic sledge smashed him out of the saddle and dropped him, breathless, in the shale of the trail.

The flat, dry crack of the shot split into fragments of sound that rolled through him and over him and off through the hills like stampeded cattle; and saddle leather creaked and a horse broke out of the brush and ran south.

15

OVERTURE TO VIOLENCE

*T*HE STAGE from Pearce was forty minutes late when it came rolling into Tucson at twenty after twelve that night and drew up with a flourish before the Cosmopolitan Hotel.

Two elegantly dressed girls, very obviously not ladies, were assisted to the ground with great ceremony and a considerable babble of eighty-five cent words by a couple of inebriated knights of the saddle.

The last person to leave the coach before it rattled down Pennington in the direction of Pearl was a man in a derby. He'd been riding the box with the driver and had a fat cigar jutting out of his mouth which he rolled across sun-chapped lips as he ogled the girls and their tipsy companions.

After a moment his green glance went beyond them, quickly scanning the front of the white-plastered one-story hostelry. Apparently satisfied, he turned and moved leisurely off toward Main with his hands in coat pockets and the smoke floating back from his fat cigar.

One of the drunken punchers stared after him. "Y' know, I sheen that dude b'fo' someplaish . . ."

The taller girl tugged at his arm. "It's the bed you was lookin' for, dearie—remember?" And the other puncher said: "Hell with 'im. Whatsa use a lookin' at a goddam dude when you gotta sweet armful like—"

"Gawd," the other girl said, "but I'm hungry! Can you get a T-bone steak in this joint?"

"Honey," Ed assured her, "you kin git ever' damn thing yore little heart desires." And they all moved off.

When Frank Esparza stepped into his office at a quarter to one, he paused with the door still open and, with shoulders hunched, stood quietly, unbreathing, with his glance grimly raking the black room before him.

"Never mind the drawn shade," said a voice from the blackness. "Come in and shut the door. An' put the lamp on, damn it. I ain't fixing to bite you."

Esparza scratched a match, found the lamp and lit it and took a long look at the man in the corner. He looked him over from yellow shoes to brown derby. Then he nodded.

"You're the dude that left town in a hell of a hurry. The coffee drummer that got the bad news and had to light out for El Paso. Did you get there?"

The man's sunburned features broke apart in a grin. "Nope. Didn't seem so necessary after I lost Cardigan. Quite a character. He been around here long?"

The marshal grunted. "Long enough to know better." He said, after a moment, "You have trouble with Cardigan?"

"I'll take care of that. I guess you'll be Frank Esparza? My name's Sollantsy—call me Sam for short." He took out his wallet, flipped it open so the marshal could see his credentials. "I'm reppin' for the Tri-State Cattlemen's Association, workin' out of Billings."

Esparza went over and sat down at his desk and hoisted his booted feet onto a drawer. "Go ahead," he said. "What's your problem?"

"Horses. Lot of our members been losin' 'em—had a regular epidemic of horse stealin' up in our neck of the woods two-three years ago. Must've lost right around about seven hundred head."

"So your members took their troubles to the Tri-State?"

"You said it," Sollantsy grinned. "They knew we'd give 'em some action. We caught a few guys and the law strung 'em up. Some of our members weren't quite satisfied though. Old R. C. Hale—he's the Tri-State's president—had been hit pretty hard. He'd been breeding some mighty top cowponies. Mostly ropers an' cutters when you got 'em finished out. He went in strong for duns an' these horse-thievin' sons seemed to take a real shine to 'em. They got twenty-five or thirty of the best, includin' Hale's top studhorse, Jubal Jo.

"We put a few men out and turned up some horses—around forty or fifty head, I reckon. Most of this stuff had been bought up by small ranchers, one or two to the spread. Took a lot of time and a lot work to find 'em, but gradually a picture began to build up. We began to catch onto how these crooks had been operatin'."

Sollantsy got a cigar from his vest and bit the end off. He went over to the lamp and puffed it into life. "The ones we had caught had mostly been locals. We had worked on a few but we didn't find out much. Most of the stuff we picked up we got in Colorado an' Utah. That showed the stuff was goin' south.

"Then one day we hit the jackpot. Following a lead we jumped a two-by-four rancher on the Colorado line. He had a place tucked away in the mountains about a hundred miles north of Estes Park. What he really had was a relay station. Stuff comin' out of our country would be driven to his place an' left to rest up. Same way with stuff bein' pushed north. He had a right sweet setup and didn't much cotton to being put out of business. He had three fellers with him an' we caught 'em flat-footed but they went for their irons an' we had to rub 'em out. We didn't get a nickel's worth of information out of 'em."

Sollantsy rolled the cigar across his mouth disgustedly. "You know how it goes. Just when you figure to bust a case wide open, along comes a shoot-out an' all you got is corpses. Stopped the stealin' though—our members ain't lost a damn horse since."

Esparza said, "Maybe that was their headquarters—"

"Not a chance," Sollantsy said. "Feller that run that place didn't have enough sense to pound sand down a rat-hole. He knew his job an' that was all. The guy that's roddin' this gang is big caliber. We don't figure the ones we've got was even members of the gang. The way we've got it doped out there probably ain't more than five or six men in the gang. All these others is extras—probably workin' for wages. They do the spottin', furnish the tips and maybe hide out the horses while they're bein' rested up. Way we've got it doped out the guys on the outside edge of this deal are mostly just scouts. All they do is get a line on good stock—where it's at, how much an' when's the best time to grab it. They pass this dope along to one of the boys in the pay of someone that's got him a relay station, and this guy passes it on to one of the gang."

"Sounds pretty complicated," Esparza commented.

"It's pretty cagey," Sollantsy nodded. "But that's one thing about Tri-State—when they fasten onto a thing they stay with it to the finish."

He puffed his cigar as though he really enjoyed it, savoring the smoke as it came out through his nostrils. "I never seen a job yet the Tri-State couldn't crack."

"Then you think they'll lick this one?"

Sollantsy grinned. "That's what I'm here for. We got it ready to scratch off the books right now."

Esparza looked at him thoughtfully. "Are you trying to tell me this gang holes up around here?"

"Within twenty miles of where we're sittin' right now."

"You've got proof of that, I reckon—"

"We got enough to turn the trick. You know how Tri-State works. We round up the evidence. We go where it takes us. When we get what we figure is enough to do the job we send in a report and contact local authorities."

Esparza nodded. "You'll be seeing the sheriff—"

"I've seen the sheriff. You got a damn big county here. Sheriff tells me he's up to his ears in work now and that you're the man to handle this end of it."

Sollantsy grinned. "He says these people around here elected you to keep down the rustling as much as anything, and that you're a bonafide deputy sheriff with full powers to go out into the county—"

"All right," Esparza said. "I can see you've got in touch with him. Who do you want me to arrest?"

"Kurt Cardigan, for a starter."

"Cardigan's a rancher, a big man around here—"

"I've looked him up. I know how big he is, an' how stand-offish. And I know what his neighbors think when they hear that tough crew he's got go by in the dark."

"That's not proof," the marshal said.

"I've got proof enough to flush him out into the open!"

"Legal murder is what you're proposing. We don't do things that way around here."

"You mean you'd coddle a horse thief—"

"Wait," Esparza said. "You don't understand the background or the issues involved—"

"I understand the law—"

"The letter of the law, perhaps. The law as it's administered in more thickly settled country. Out here it's a little different. We try to temper justice with a little bit of mercy. Laws are conceived and passed to hold down crime and—"

"I know all that!"

Esparza smiled patiently. "I want you to get the picture in its proper proportions. If Cardigan's a horse thief I'm not condoning his actions or proposing to ignore them. I've heard the same rumors you have and I've gone to a lot of work trying to dig out the truth. Though I've found no proof I could take to a jury, I'm pretty well convinced in my own mind he was stealing horses up north and selling them later as stock of his own raising—"

"Then what the hell you waitin' on?"

"Proof," the marshal said stubbornly.

Sollantsy took the cigar from his mouth and said harshly: "I've got all the proof we need! That guy run me out of this town at gun point. He was so hellbent to get rid of me he bought me a horse at Reagan's livery, a dun filly with a white mane and tail that I happen to know was raised by Bob Hale at Big Timber, Montana—one of the horses he lost to this bunch of damn horse thieves! An' that ain't all by a long shot! That stallion Cardigan rides around is Jubal Jo, Hale's top studhorse!"

He got his cigar going again and said grimly, "I've been out to Camp Grant lookin' over some of that stuff he pushed off on the cavalry. I didn't turn up a thing I could put the finger on but there's a lot of their horses I didn't get to see. If you want to force my hand I'll go back there, but why fiddle

around? You handle this right an' we'll get all the proof anybody will ask for."

"Sure," Esparza nodded. "Bullet proof."

"What's the matter with that?" Sollantsy bristled.

"It's not the way we do business—"

"It's results that count, not the way you get 'em. When
you're dealin' with a horse thief—"

"You figure when Cardigan's bunch sees a posse comin'
they'll either break and run or start throwing lead. Either way
they're guilty accordin' to your book. They're guilty before
you ever start after them. You're not stopping to count the
cost in misery and dead men or the chance that Cardigan
might happen to be innocent—"

Sollantsy snorted. "If that guy's innocent I'm a sidewinder's
uncle!"

"Not innocent perhaps of stealing Jubal Jo, but he could
very well be innocent of the things that have been going on
around here since then."

Sollantsy stared. "So now you're splittin' hairs! What kind
of a setup have I walked into? How much of a graft are you
gettin' from this guy?"

Esparza said quietly, "You have to realize the powerful in-
fluence of this country. This isn't Texas or Kansas or even
Montana; the laws of those sections do not fit into our problems. They do not fit our conditions or these peculiar times.
We're in transition, Sollantsy. This country puts its mark on
every man who tries to live here—it actually does this, bringing out in him swiftly—even oftentimes magnifying—whatever
tendencies he has toward either good or evil.

"It is a big, tough country and it's always attracted a pretty
rough kind of man. Weakness is not always just a matter of
muscle; there can be weakness of character, too, Sollantsy,
and many weak characters have come into this country, and
the effect of this country on them has generally been unfor-
tunate. Such men, if they survive, very frequently become outlaws—"

"Hell!" Sollantsy sneered, "I didn't come to your office to
listen to no sermon—"

"I'm trying to show you why your suggested method of handling Cardigan is wrong," Esparza said. "Let us admit for the record that Cardigan has deliberately acquired brandless horses that did not belong to him—let us even go so far as to admit that this is stealing. At the time in question—the time you fellers up north were losing horses—a great many men were doing the same thing in cattle, and were considered none the worse for it. Some of these mavericks became cattle barons—"

"We've passed laws against it—"

"We didn't pass them here until just a couple of months ago. Since that time you have no proof whatever that Cardigan hasn't been completely on the square."

"You sure do love that guy, don't you?"

"He could be a very useful citizen and I think he's trying to reform," Esparza said.

"He should've done his reformin' before he run off with them horses." The Tri-States man knocked the ashes off his smoke. "If you think Bob Hale is gonna forget Jubal Jo—"

"I think I can handle that part of it. I believe Cardigan will pay a good price for that horse, and for everything else that came out of your country—"

"Well, buddy, I'm glad to meet up with you," Sollantsy said, with his hard bright eyes going over Esparza carefully. "I thought your kind had all died in the Crusades."

"Don't you believe in giving a man a break?"

"Not no goddam horse thief! All I've got for his kind of skunk is a rope thrown over a juniper branch."

Esparza said quietly, "We'll have none of that here."

"Are you tellin' me you refuse to take action? If you think Tri-States—"

"I'm not thinking about Tri-States at all. I'm thinking of a man who may be trying to go straight, and of the probable results to this country if such a man happened to be pushed the wrong way."

He took his feet off the desk and picked up his hat. "An ounce of prevention can be worth a pound of cure. We've had a bad outbreak of violence in this Territory during the last couple of weeks," he told Sollantsy softly. "I don't think Cardigan's mixed up in it, but I *do* think he may help to put a stop to it and perhaps recover some of the money that's been stolen—if he's given half a chance."

He considered the other man steadily. "I may be setting a thief to catch a thief, but in my book it's a form of prevention and I intend to stay with it until I see what it can do."

The bright green stare of the Tri-States man showed a plain and bitter outrage. "Then you aim to keep settin' right here on your fanny—that's what you're tryin' to tell me, ain't it?"

"I intend, first of all, to try and get back the loot that was taken from the Copper State Bank and the bank at Douglas," Frank Esparza said mildly. "I've sent a deputy down there to look things over and I shall wait for his report. If that report should show definite evidence against Cardigan or if, in the meantime, Cardigan appears to have ignored the warning I gave him, I shall then be ready to consider other measures."

Cardigan stayed where he was in the shale of the trail until the last flogging hoofbeat of that horse had faded out. He felt, during those moments, no pain at all; he felt only the shock and a strange frightening numbness that seemed to encompass the whole left side of his chest.

He knew his chances of getting up were a lot better now than they would be later after the numbness wore off. He twisted over on his side and drew one leg up. It astonished him to find that it could take him so long.

Getting shot this way was no one's fault but his own. A man who had tampered with the law as long as he had should have known a heap better than to ride through moonlight on a giveaway horse. Hadn't he given the crew hell for stealing Snuffy in the first place? And hadn't Lahr told him the horse would get him killed?

He got a knee under him and gathered his strength. What was it Rickven had said about someone before him? Someone going too fast for him to hail the man down. A pity, by God, he hadn't thought of this sooner. Or at least kept his eyes peeled. He was in a hell of a shape now to do what had to be done.

He staggered up with a groan and almost fell down again. He stood there, dizzy and giddy for several moments, feeling exhausted beyond the strength it took to move—but that was crazy. He had to move. He *had* to. He had to get to the ranch, though he couldn't remember why.

He tried to whistle for Snuffy, but his whistler wouldn't work. His mind wasn't working too damned good, either. What he needed was some action, something to get him woke up. He said: "I got to get out of here."

He tried to whistle again but finally gave it up. He tried to think where he was, looking wearily about him, but he couldn't seem to get up much enthusiasm for it. Thing to do was start walking. He started.

It gave him a weird kind of funny sensation, like he didn't have any connection with the ground—like he was a bird or a balloon or something. His feet didn't seem to have any weight, or the ground beneath him to have any substance. Sometimes he didn't hardly know whether he had his feet hoisted up or down; but after a while it seemed they must have turned to lead and it was all he could do to even drag them along after him.

But he knew where he was now, five miles beyond Rickven's in the Bent Creek bottoms. Less than a mile to the house. He wondered if he'd make it.

And then feeling came back and pain stabbed through him like a saw-edged sword. It came in waves that left him shaking but he kept on going. Sometimes he cursed the bushwhacker who had tried to dry-gulch him, but more often he cursed himself that he should have been so damn careless. If he'd had enough sense to drive nails in a snowbank he might have guessed someone would try this. It was the obvious thing to look for if the crew had doublecrossed him and stuck up those two banks.

One of them, of course, might have been in town tonight and seen him chinning with the marshal. But if the crew had robbed those banks—which was what Esparza had hinted—it was fifty-seven to one that Shiloh Frayne or Curly Lahr had got fed up with two-bit stakes and decided to take the lid off. And if this was how the thing had gone, the next step, of necessity, was to rid the gang of Kurt.

He remembered then that the horse had gone south, had gone crashing off in the direction of town; and he shook his head and gave it up. If someone in town had got an urge to waylay him there were a hundred places handier than this. No feller from town would have come way out here in the middle of the night. It was one of the crew, that was all there was to it; and when he got home and saw the horses he'd know.

He concentrated on getting there.

But he couldn't keep from thinking.

His gun was still wedged in the waistband of his trousers and he was damn glad it was because there wasn't much doubt he'd need it.

He wished the hell his mind would take a rest, but it kept going round like a wound-up clock, like the whirlpool down in the Broken Bit narrows, always churning up things that he'd just as lief stayed buried. Like his childhood on the south Texas ranch, an endless miserable stretch of back-breaking labor because his old man had been too tight to hire the help the outfit needed. When most kids his age had been going to school he'd had to ride fence, break broncs and tail bogged steers up. A hell of a happy time he'd had; and the two years they'd made his old man send him hadn't been much better. The kids had laughed their heads off to see a guy so big so goddam dumb.

He'd run away finally, thinking to improve his lot, but all he'd found was work and more of it; and trouble, of course— he'd always found trouble. He remembered the cook on the XIT, the wagon boss on the Diamond A, the strayman at the Gourd and Vine. Then he'd tried his hand at freighting and a rival line had wrecked half his wagons and he'd beat the boss up and had to quit the country.

He recalled his first gun fight, one of the few chunks of trouble he hadn't brought on himself; and a girl he had known in Corpus Christi, and that fetched his mind back to Docie. Docie Balinett who was waiting for him now; and suddenly he felt he couldn't take another step.

But he did. He scowled into the silver-dappled shadows and kept on tramping with the stubborn tenacity that was the most enduring thing he'd ever got from the Cardigans; and finally the ranch lights threw their yellow beacons through the interlacing branches of the cottonwoods and catclaw.

He did not find it queer that any lights would still be showing. He was remembering all at once the look on Rickven's hangdog features when he'd asked him what a sheriff would do if he had the real dirt on a rustler. There'd been something almost furtive, almost frightened in that look. There'd been sweat on Rickven's cheekbones and something in his voice that, now he thought it over, bordered mighty close on panic.

And then he remembered Esparza, and it came to Kurt like a bolt from the blue what had put that look on the nester's face. It was Rickven, that Kurt had let squat on his land, who had tipped Frank Esparza off!

The knowledge stopped Cardigan dead in his tracks. He forgot where he was, forgot all the pain in his sudden black fury; and he was that way, half turned and half minded to go back, when a girl's frantic cry swung his face toward the house.

16

A VERY POTENT QUESTION

*W*HEN Top Hat Charlie drove the hired rig into the yard at Cardigan's KC ranch headquarters, the girl who shared its seat was not feigning astonishment when she said, looking about her with an intake of breath, "Are you sure this is the place?"

"Quite." The Englishman's nod held only a studied civility.

"But, Charlie, it's *big!*" Docie cried, with her gray-green glance wholly approving the arrangement of the sturdy log buildings scattered among the trees. "I'd no idea he had a place like this."

"A matter of some three hundred thousand acres, I believe. Not patented, of course—just held. . . ." He seemed about to say more but let it go with a shrug. "Yes, it's big," he said cryptically—"big as Cardigan himself, and just about as vulnerable, given the right set of circumstances."

Docie turned her head to regard him. "You think Cardigan's vulnerable?"

"Like glass."

"I'm not sure I understand."

"You will if you stay around here." He leaned toward her impulsively. "I'm concerned for you, Docie. Chuck this, won't you? Let me take you back to town—"

"It's too late for that, Charlie."

"It's not too late yet. Look. There's nobody here—"

"They're probably in the house."

"Look at the corrals. No horses in them. Let me—"

"You *are* sweet, Charlie. Perhaps you're right in not liking Cardigan, but it just wouldn't work. This isn't a thing I've gone into rashly."

"I'm afraid it is," he answered quietly. "It's something you're doing on the rebound, Docie. You can't run away from things. Believe me. You can run to the very ends of the earth but the thing you would escape remains as near you as your shadow."

"But I'm not running, Charlie. There's nothing in my past that I'm ashamed of. Regret—being sorry for a thing isn't necessarily shame. I have made my mistakes but I'm not running from them. I want a different kind of life."

"Did you find the old so bad?"

"I want trust and security. I want a set of values I can depend on. When I see a thing that's white I want it always to remain that way. I am tired of sham and shifting shadows. I want to feel that I matter—I want security, Charlie."

"Nevertheless, you will not find it. You will never find it

here. You don't know the man you are trying to do business with."

Docie said, breathing deep: "I would rather belong to one honest rustler—"

"It isn't that."

"What is it then?"

Charlie spread his hands in a gambler's gesture. "The man has built a house of cards. A strong wind is gathering. When this house falls down I would not like to see you pinned underneath it. Believe me, Docie, there's no future in Cardigan."

She looked a long moment at his handsome face, seeing how the evening breeze ruffled the silvering hair at his temples, noticing now how gray he had become in the years since those carefree days at San Saba. But she had put the past behind her and she meant to keep it there.

He said: "I think—" and paused to look at her sharply; and he shook his head and let the rest go and put his thin lips together, locking his thoughts away behind the impassive look he customarily wore while taking his turn at the Gold Plate Saloon.

"We all have our own lives to live," Docie said. "A woman takes the best she can get—"

"All right," he said. "At least you can wait for Cardigan in town. Get a room at the Cosmopolitan or Palace."

Something in her eyes silently thanked him, but she said, "I will wait for him here," and he helped her down in the hard bright sunlight and fetched her bag from under the seat.

She knew suddenly, watching him, that here was a lonely man; and then he turned his head and caught the reflection of that thought on her face.

"Good luck." He smiled and lifted his head, and climbed into the buggy and drove away.

They had been like two ships that, going in opposite directions, meet and pass in the ocean. Like the ships, so alone against the vast panorama of sky and water, they had a certain routine and their aloneness in common; nothing more. She halfway wished, for Charlie's sake, they might have found their destiny beneath the same star, for she was a full-bodied woman, rich in all those things for which a man eternally searches; and there was much in the Englishman that she could admire.

A sadness touched her lips and she sighed. A person never should look back.

She picked up the bag and started for the house, a substantial looking place with curtains at the windows; but partway across the yard she stopped, struck by the incongruity of a feminine touch peeping out of a structure that looked more like a fortress than it did a stockman's ranch house.

Curtains at the windows.

It didn't fit anything she'd heard about Cardigan.

"Hello," she called. "Hello! Hello!" came the echo.

With a shrug she went on. The massive door stood open and she paused beside it, listening; and it seemed to listen with her.

She smiled at that and, setting down her bag, went in.

Notwithstanding the curtained windows, the place looked masculine enough in all conscience. This was the living room apparently, an immense and lofty barn of a place with an enormous fireplace at the far end. The walls were unfinished pine sheeting. Dark furniture was set about the walls and a massive table made a dark and uncompromising island in the center of the room. Indian rugs were scattered splashes of color against the yellow boards of the floor. There was a lamp with a round glass shade on the table and a handful of brass-jacketed cartridges that flung back the blaze of the lowering sun. Chairs that were barrel-shaped lattices of parti-colored slats with hide stretched over their upper framework were set about at regular intervals; there was a saddle in one, a pair of saddlebags in another and the rest were draped with discarded sweat-stained clothing. And a buff-colored dust powdered everything.

Docie shook her head. It was time Kurt Cardigan got himself a woman if this was a sample of the rest of the house.

And it was. The kitchen was cluttered with dirty dishes. There was a bed in one room with no bedclothes on it, a cracked pitcher and basin. A chest of drawers had another room all to itself. There was nothing soft in the entire place but the curtains.

With spirits somewhat dampened Docie returned to the living room and was trying to make up her mind if she should pitch in and clean it when the sound of approaching hoofbeats drew her glance to the door.

A rider came into her line of vision, a hard-faced fellow in the garb of a cowboy. She watched him ride into the corral and dismount with an irritable mumble that had the sound of profanity. She noticed that he limped as he set about unsaddling. She watched him turn the horse loose and hang his saddle on a pole, afterwards leaving the pen and coming toward the house, still muttering.

She wondered if this were Cardigan and went reluctantly outside to meet him.

He seemed too busy with his thoughts to notice her. He was a gangling, loose-shackled specimen who looked seven shades rougher than hell itself. Midway of the yard he swung left toward a long narrow building that had a bench outside it on which reposed one bent pail and a rusty basin.

He must have felt her looking at him for he spun round of a sudden with his hand flashing hipward. He had his gun clear of leather before he got a good look at her. You could see realization hit him in the way his jaw sagged and the way he went rigid.

Docie said: "Is Mr. Cardigan here?"

"Who the hell are you?"

"My name is Balinett. I'm looking for Kurt Cardigan. I—he's expecting me."

"First I heard of it. First I heard of you, either," he said, putting his gun up, but with his face still hostile. His eyes kept boring into her. "You musta got off on the wrong foot or somethin'—he don't want no women around this place. Them's his orders. No women. You better pick up that bag an' head back where you come from."

Docie looked at him coolly. "I believe I'll just wait."

"Wrong guess," he said. "Get that bag an' get outa here."

She shook her head, meeting his look with that direct way

she had while their wills clashed and locked and a dark surge of color crept above his open collar.

He said, loud and angry: "Do you know what kind of a place this is?"

"It's a horse ranch, isn't it?"

"You didn't come out here to buy no horse."

"No." She smiled a little then. "I came out here because Mr. Cardigan sent for me."

She could see him turning it over, could see he didn't believe her. She said, "He sent me the money to come here."

He didn't believe that at all and didn't like it. He closed his jaws so tight it brought a scar out lividly the length of his chin. The black look of his eyes became more unreasoning and a kind of violence beat through him, making her draw back a little.

He said, "You're wastin' your time."

Docie's cheeks showed a touch of color. "After all," she said, "I'm the best judge of that—"

"You fool," he cried bitterly. "The man's gone—pulled his freight! He don't live here any more!"

"Nevertheless, I shall wait," Docie told him and, ignoring the outraged look of him, turned and went back into the house.

Three-quarters of an hour later she had the living room looking as though people lived there. All the dust was swept out and all the clothes and gear picked up and put into the room with the chest of drawers. In the drawers she had found a couple of clean blankets which she put on the bed. Then she fetched in her bag and started in on the kitchen.

By the time she had it looking as a kitchen ought to look she was ravenously hungry. The feeling was probably accentuated by the tantalizing odors of a cooking meal that were emanating now from the long skinny building into which her surly interrogator had gone. He was probably the cook; which was one blessing anyway. At least she wouldn't have to cook her own supper.

While she was waiting for him to call her, she decided to

clean up. What with trail grime and house grime she felt dirty all over.

She went into the other room and got clean underthings and a fresh dress from her bag and brought them back into the kitchen, laying them on one of the recently scrubbed chairs. She put another chair under the knob of the door. She really needed some hot water but she didn't feel like bothering to build a fire to get some. Cold water from the well would have to do, she reckoned, and proceeded to pump the sink full. At least there was plenty of soap, great brown blocks of it stacked on a shelf.

She looked around at the windows, of which there were two; one above the sink and a bigger one back of the stove. The one above the sink faced the yard. The other one was in the back wall of the room and gave out on a wide sweep of grass covered hills that were yellow from long drought. There were no shades at either window, and no curtains. There were solid slabs of board that could be closed across the windows but she didn't feel like going to all the bother of that. The cook was getting supper and had made it very plain he wasn't interested in women.

She pulled off her dress and got out of her crumpled underthings. Sometimes, she thought irrelevantly, it must be nice to be an Indian. She got a wash cloth from her bag and a big soft fuzzy towel. She laid the towel on the drain-board and put the wash cloth in the water. It was then that she remembered she didn't have anything to stand in.

Should she get the cracked pitcher and basin from the bedroom? She looked out into the yard which, as before, was hotly empty. She could hear the cook banging around in his shanty. She really wanted that basin. It would only take a moment. With a shrug, she decided to risk it and pulled the chair from beneath the knob.

She crossed the long living room, the yellow boards of the floor feeling warm beneath her feet. Moving into the bedroom she lifted the heavy pitcher and got the basin out from under. Turning then, she caught the reflection of her sunlit shape in the window and paused a moment, not entirely satisfied.

It was nothing to be ashamed of. A little slim, perhaps, but adequately rounded in the most appropriate places. It had never been her fortune though she knew it could have been.

She was halfway across the living room when the sound of men's voices startled her. She flew into the kitchen most becomingly flushed, whipped the towel around her and got the spare chair beneath the doorknob again. Then she took a deep breath and cautiously peeked out the window that was over the sink.

There was another horse in the yard. Still saddled, it stood on dangling reins before the cabin where the man who didn't like women was rattling pots and pans. By the mutter of voices both men were in there, but their talk was more unintelligible here than it had been in the other room.

Leaning forward, Docie raised the window a little. She still couldn't hear what the two men were saying.

Fearing any moment they might call her to supper or, worse, that one of them might come to fetch her personally, she hurried through her bath and got into her clothes. A girl liked to spend a little time with her bath—it was bad enough having to take it standing in a basin—but she couldn't afford much dawdling with a couple of unattached males on the premises.

Hastily combing out her hair, she put it up without brushing and supposed she looked a sight but there was nothing she could do about it. Cardigan, apparently, had never found the need of investing in a mirror.

She looked out the back window. The sun was dropping behind the hills and, already, the shadows were turning purple-black. She wished that cook would shake it up a little. She could have cooked supper twice in this length of time.

She picked up her discarded clothes and carried them into the room where she'd put all the stuff she'd picked up in the living room. Then she went back and tidied the kitchen and took the basin back into the bedroom. She couldn't see her reflection in the window now. . . .

After a while she went back in the living room and sat

down in one of the hide-bottomed chairs; the dry leather creaked abysmally but she found it surprisingly comfortable. The vast silence of this country seemed to reach all through the house. A pleasant lassitude stole over her, a peace she hadn't known in months.

It was dark when she realized the cook wasn't going to call her. Really dark. She could see the winking gleam of stars through the lesser black of the open door. She had no idea how long she'd been dozing; it must have been a good while.

She got up and went to the door and stood a moment looking out. The whole yard was dark and the foliaged branches of the trees made great patches of blackness against the deep blue of the star-girded night. The men were sitting on the bench before the cookshack. She could hear their occasional movements and, now and again, the desultory murmur of their voices; she could see the fitful glow of one man's cigarette.

So they had eaten their supper and now were smoking, taking their ease, and neither of them had bothered to give her a call. Surely horsethief hospitality had little to recommend it.

She wondered what time it was getting to be, and abruptly realized she hadn't seen a clock since she'd come into this house. No clock and no mirror. Cardigan certainly needed some lessons in housekeeping.

Groping her way to the kitchen she got a match from the box hanging back of the stove. She stood a while then, carefully thinking things over; but finally, with a shrug, she scratched her match and lit the bracket lamp appended to the kitchen's back wall. Then she got another match and went back and lit the lamp on the living room table.

The voices of the two men were louder now; lifted in some kind of altercation. But she paid them no attention. What she wanted now was to get some food inside her. She hated like sin having to fix her own supper, but she hated even worse the thought of going to bed hungry.

She was glad she had put on this gingham dress; it was cooler than the taffeta and a lot more comfortable. She was not a bit sorry she'd done her cleaning in the other. Taffeta, someway, seemed out of place around here.

She looked out the door. A silver moon was coming up. The men seemed to be having some kind of an argument. She heard the cook say plainly: "You kin be a goddam fool if you want to, but I don't want no part of it!" And she went back to the kitchen to see what a search of the curtained shelves would turn up.

It didn't turn up much in the way of food. A couple of boxes of biscuits the rats had been into, three still-unopened cans of sardines, three Bermuda onions, a sack of dried beans, a ten-pound bag of salt and a scant half sack of weevilly flour.

Docie turned away with a grimace.

She'd rather go to bed hungry than to ask a man like that cook for anything. Nor did she very much relish the thought of going to bed. It wasn't that she was afraid exactly, but . . .

Supposing the cook had told the truth about Cardigan? If Charlie's gambling house rumors had been based on anything stronger than jaw-wagging . . . She recalled then what the cook had said first and felt better. *He don't want no women around here. Them's his orders—no women.* He'd not have opened up that way if Cardigan had gone.

But why would Cardigan have given such an order?

Hoof sound turned her face toward the window and a kind of excitement brightened her cheeks. She would soon have all her doubts set at rest; surely this was Cardigan coming now. What would he be like? And what would he think of her? Would she suit him—would she be the kind of woman he was hoping and expecting?

Well, why not? Not an inconsiderable number of the men she had known, including Top Hat Charlie, would have felt themselves fortunate to get a woman like her. She didn't guess Kurt Cardigan would be much different from the rest; at least, so far as what he wanted was concerned.

She tried to see out the window but the light in the room threw back too many reflections. She heard a jingle of spur chains and went hurrying into the living room to pull up with an unaccustomed fluster when she saw the man in the open door. It hadn't occurred to her before that she might not like Cardigan.

He stood in scuffed boots with big-roweled spurs and his long legs were covered with brush-clawed chaps. There was a glisten of sweat on his hard burnt face and his thumbs were hooked in a heavy black belt that gleamed with cartridges and held a bone handled gun in a tied-down holster. His chin-strapped hat was broad-brimmed and low of crown and a grin pulled thick lips from his tobacco stained teeth.

"Hello there, honey. Reckon it's been pretty lonesome fer you hangin' around here."

"I finally got here."

"Yeah. Sure—sure you did." He came into the room and she felt frozen in her tracks. "Sure you did." He grinned, and stood there, looking at her.

He had yellow, lashless eyes that were unwinking as a snake's.

She felt she had to say something. "What—what took you so long?"

"That goddam cook. I had t' git rid of him. Didn't even know you was here till we got all done with eatin'—sometimes I don't think that guy's got 'em all."

He grinned at her again. "I bet you're hungrier'n a bear."

It was this consideration, this reminder of her hunger, that threw her off guard. He got his arms around her before she knew what was happening. He covered her mouth with his. With a furious effort she wrenched herself free and stood back from him, panting.

There was surprise on his face. "Gosh, honey," he said, with contrition, "I didn't reckon t' scare you—Christ, I wouldn't scare you fer anythin'! Guess I never expected you would be so danged beautiful. . . . I—I guess I jest sorta broke plumb away from myself." His voice came down a notch. "I—I'm sure sorry if I was rough."

Docie felt for a chair and dropped into it suddenly, feeling weak as a kitten.

She didn't know what to do, or what to say or what to think. He *did* look sorry. She guessed she was acting like a fool but she hadn't been prepared for anything like this. Mostly these cowboys were shy, timid fellows when they got around a woman. She had forgotten how wild they could sometimes be.

She just stared at him, wondering. She felt all tangled up inside. She didn't know whether she wanted to laugh or to cry. After all, she'd come out here of her own free will to marry him. If he had been a little precipitate wasn't it probably no more than natural when you considered the kind of life he led, the lonesomeness of it, the hard work and danger?

She lifted a hand and pushed back her hair. She took a deep breath and tried to smile at him. "I—I'll be all right in a minute."

"Sure."

She put out her hand so that he could help her up.

"Sure you will." He grinned, and came over and took it.

She knew, too late, she'd made another mistake. His hand closed around hers like a bear trap. As it pulled her onto her feet his other hand came forward and tore the front of her dress loose. Then he had her in his arms again and was bending her backward with his mouth crushed tight on hers. She tried to get his gun but he slapped her hand away; and she could feel him laughing deep down in his throat as he caught her overbalanced weight against his thigh.

She twisted her head and got her mouth free and screamed.

He laughed openly now, exultantly.

"Go ahead—yell. The cook's rode off. Who the hell you think'll hear you?"

She could feel the hot breath of him against her cheek. She tried again to break loose and he bent an arm behind her, twisting till she quit. There was a roaring in her ears, a sound of running feet. The hot, gloating, bright yellow eyes were gone off focus. She was like a swimmer going under for the third and final time when she heard a man's voice quietly say:

"Don't you reckon you've gone about far enough, Frayne?"

17

DANGEROUS BUSINESS

*S*HE HAD no trouble getting clear of him now. His shape was still as though turned to stone and all the steel was gone out of his fingers. They still gripped her arms but there was no strength in them and she tore herself from them, staggering back against the support of the table.

Only then did she see the other man, the one whose voice had set her free. He was by the open outside door, a yellow-haired man in trail-grimed garb with a spatter of dust streaked across granite features. There was blood on his shirt and his cheeks looked ghastly but a hard smile twisted his saturnine lips.

"Turn around, you cheap tinhorn, and let's have a look at a skunk on two legs."

All the flush of hot blood had fallen out of Frayne's face. And all the boldness. There was not much difference between his tawny eyes now and the painted glass buttons tied into the head of the elk above the mantel.

"Turn around," the man said, and Frayne did so, stiffly.

He tried to shake himself together. He licked parched lips and life crept cautiously into his eyes and sent ragged glances this way and that like the eyes of a weasel backed into a corner. It wasn't a pretty thing to see.

But the man in the doorway wasn't pretty either with that blood all over the front of his shirt, with his cheeks so gray and glance so bitter. He was like a man skewered above the fires of hell. It was his calm, she thought, that made him seem so alarming. Whatever it was, you could not fail to be conscious of this man's deadly power. It was an aura about him, a suggestion of violence held in leash by a hair.

"What do you reckon will be the end of you, Frayne?"

Frayne flushed and scowled. He appeared to have gotten

back some of his assurance and there was, just back of those yellow eyes, intermingled with the fright, an arousing anger compounded of thwarted passion and injured pride. You could see it gnawing him, burning like acid across all those barriers of care and caution flung about him by the look of this other man's eyes. You could see it battling with the fright that was in him: but the fright was strongest and it shaped his answer.

"Hell! I thought you an' me was friends, Kurt."

Kurt! Docie stiffened. So *this* was Cardigan, this yellow-haired man! A deep breath lifted the swell of her breasts and she looked at him carefully.

He was a solid shape with the look of hard living ground into his features. The scars of his trade had left their marks on him in the high-voltage look of his saturnine eyes, in the lines around his mouth, in the whole appearance of him. Here was no man to be dismissed with a tag. A tremendous energy was in this man, a dynamic something that colored his every look and gesture; a quietness that bordered on insolence.

"Friends, eh? Was you thinkin' of that when you was maulin' this woman?"

"Hell's fire! I wa'n't maulin' her—"

"What was you doin'?"

Frayne threw out his hands. "I was jest sorta honey-fussin' round with her a little—"

"Do you always tear their dresses when you're honey-fussin' round?"

Cardigan's words flung a bright color into Frayne's face. Stung pride and resentment worked their yeasty way through him and he blew out a gust of breath and cried wildly: "You got no call to be ridin' herd on me! I knew this skirt when she was up at Dodge City—"

"She ain't up at Dodge City now," Cardigan said. And his eyes grew darker as he stared at the man. "You know my rules about women. Get on your horse and ride out of here. An' don't bother to fetch yourself back."

Frayne stood perfectly still. Then he shook his shoulders

together and the resentful, corrosive rage that was in him burned through to his cheeks and he yelled in a high half-strangled voice, "You can't kick me off like a empty boot! By God, I got some rights around here!"

A cold grin tugged the set of Cardigan's lips. "Sure you have. You got a gun in your belt. If you want to fight for 'em, use it."

Frayne's eyes came wide open.

He went back half a step, and then he went back another. All the anger fell out of his face and left it ashen.

"You want your rights." Cardigan sneered. "Go on an' pull it."

Sweat made a shine along the side of Frayne's cheeks. A moment ago he'd been a bundle of fury. Rage and resentment had obscured his judgment, blinding him to where his wild words might take him. Now he found himself shaking.

He could no more have lifted that gun off his hip than he could have scratched his right ear with his own left elbow.

"Just a fourflusher, eh?" Cardigan taunted. "I reckoned all the yeller wasn't used up in your eyes. Toss your gun on the table—an' if you wanta die quick hit the lamp an' I'll oblige you."

With a ludicrous care Frayne did as commanded.

Cardigan shook his head, dissatisfied. "By Gawd, but you're a beauty. Plumb cultus!" He sneered.

Frayne said nothing at all. He closed his heavy jaws and kept his thoughts to himself.

Cardigan said: "Pick up your gun."

"What's that for?" Frayne said, making no move to go near it.

"I like you better with a gun in your fist. You don't look so much like a rabbit."

"I'll get by."

"Pick it up!" Cardigan said.

Frayne's malign stare licked at Cardigan darkly. He never lifted a finger, never moved from his tracks.

"What's the matter? You froze there?"

"Do I look crazy?" Frayne sneered.

"You look like a woman-baitin', white-livered sneak that ain't got enough guts to take a slap at a sand flea. I reckon I could take a batch of corn shucks an' lightnin' bugs an' make you run till your tongue flopped out like a calf rope. You musta lost all your sand tryin' t' best my woman—Christ!" Cardigan snarled, "ain't there nothin' I kin say that'll put a spark to your powder?"

Frayne's cheeks were the color of butcher paper but he kept his hands stiffly held in plain view. It was no great feat to guess what line his thoughts were taking. There was not much fear in his tawny eyes now; they were baleful and hating and scheming out a course that he might take some other day.

It was plain enough to Docie. Frayne had shed his fright with that gun; he was gambling that Cardigan would not shoot an unarmed man.

She amended that conclusion after considering him a moment. Shiloh Frayne wasn't gambling; he was confident Kurt wouldn't shoot him and, considering his former agitation, he could only have one basis for such confidence—the fact that his gun was in plain sight on yonder table.

But, if Cardigan had ever entertained the thought of killing him, why had he disarmed Shiloh Frayne in the first place? He hadn't disarmed Frayne actually; he had told Frayne to toss his gun on the table. A mistake?

Looking at Cardigan Docie didn't think so. She thought it much more likely he had wanted Frayne to draw; that Cardigan's deliberate intention had been to put a gun in Frayne's hand in the hope Frayne would try to use it.

But Frayne had been too frightened. He had not risen to Cardigan's bait. And now he saw Cardigan's purpose and would not go anywhere near the gun.

Even Cardigan seemed to know the chance was lost. He looked at Frayne with a biting contempt. "Get up on your hind feet, skunk, an' git outa here. I'm goin' to have my woman blow out the lamp an' fetch me that rifle over there

on them elk horns. If you know when you're lucky you won't
be doin' no stoppin' till you've got yourself clean on outa the
country. Go on now—git!"

18

INTERRUPTED JOURNEY

*I*N THE darkness of the room after the lamp
in the kitchen also had been snuffed and she had fetched
Kurt Cardigan the rifle off the elk horns, Docie did what she
could to repair the bodice of her dress. But her fingers seemed
all thumbs and she kept remembering the grip of Shiloh
Frayne's hands. She had never felt so terribly alone and de-
fenseless.

She looked to where Cardigan stood in the doorway, a
solid black shape with a rifle, watching Frayne's progress
across the bright yard. This was the man she had come here
to marry, the man with whom she had hoped to find security;
but the sight of him standing there failed to reassure her,
and she shivered again, thinking into the future.

After all, what did she know of him?

Even remembrance of his forbearance in the matter of
Shiloh Frayne did not greatly brighten her outlook; she had
a disquieting conviction there'd been something about that
business which she had not fully grasped.

What kind of man was he underneath that grim exterior?

She thought now that perhaps she had been a little hasty
in turning down Charlie's suggestion that she go back and
do her waiting for Cardigan in town. Supposing he were to
treat her as Frayne had? She'd come here of her own accord.
He was a bigger man than Shiloh Frayne and a rougher one
by the look of him. Suppose he didn't care to wait for any
marriage lines? He had told her very bluntly that what he
wanted was a woman.

And there was Frayne. Who could say what any man might do after coming on her and Frayne the way he had?

She remembered the icy blaze of his eyes.

St. Louis, of a sudden, seemed a very desirable place.

She felt an uprush of panic, an almost overpowering urge to run away and lose herself in the yellow grass of the wind-swept hills. She had to bite her lower lip to keep it from trembling.

She was moving with stealthy care in the direction of the kitchen when the sound of Frayne's departing horse brought her to her senses. She must quit this foolish nonsense. She'd come out here to marry Kurt Cardigan; she mustn't let the thought of Frayne unsettle her in this fashion. All he'd actually done had been to steal a couple of kisses; his ultimate intentions had nothing to do with reality. Because Frayne had been a beast was no good reason for thinking Cardigan one. The only thing she knew of Kurt was definitely in his favor. Though under great provocation and with ample opportunity he hadn't been able to bring himself to shoot an unarmed man.

She turned her head for another look at him, and caught her breath sharply as she found herself staring at an unbroken rectangle of moonlit yard. The black shape of Cardigan was no longer in the door.

She fought down a wild impulse to scream. There must be some explanation, some perfectly natural reason . . .

She went hurrying forward, almost plunging headlong when her foot rammed into something soft and yielding. Even before she heard his groan she knew, with a sudden sick remembrance of that blood on his shirt, that this was Cardigan.

She found the sulphur matches and got the living room lamp lit. She wouldn't let herself think as she brought the lamp over and put it down beside Cardigan. She was afraid now—really afraid with a cold and sinking feeling that was creeping all through her. She knew she mustn't give way to it. His life—perhaps her own, might well depend on what she did now.

She had had some experience with wounds; her father had been a doctor, though much too frank for the good of his family.

Cardigan lay sprawled just inside the open door; he seemed more to have slid down the wall than to have fallen. She dropped to her knees beside him, steeling herself against the sight of his wound. Very carefully she opened and folded back the grimy shirt.

The lonesome sounds of the night drifted in; she heard the distant rush of the wind. *Keep cool*, she told herself. *You've got to keep cool.*

But when she looked at his chest the breath caught in her throat. She must have hot water. She remembered the salt on the curtained shelf and hurried to build up a fire in the stove. She put on a big pot of water.

While she was waiting for it to boil she went back and again looked at Cardigan, worriedly. She ought to get him on a bed; she felt distrustful of her ability. She was a long way from puny, even when judged by current standards which seemed inclined to weigh a woman after the manner of a heifer, but she doubted that her strength would prove sufficient to lift Cardigan. He was a pile of man any way you looked at him.

And it sure wouldn't do to go dragging him around. By the looks of that wound he was due for a fever.

He was probably better off left right there on the floor.

She fetched a clean petticoat from her bag and tore it into strips for bandaging. The pot of water on the stove was beginning to boil and she stirred in some salt from the bag on the shelf. When she judged it had boiled a sufficient length of time she lifted it off and took it into the living room. Cardigan was groaning but was still unconscious.

She went back and washed her hands and returned with the spoon she had used to stir the salt. Dropping two of her cloths in the steaming mixture she twirled them around till she felt sure they were disinfected and then fished one out and held it on the spoon until the steam went out of it.

Carefully then, she washed the clotted blood away from the

ugly hole. She got him on his side and pulled the shirt up over his back. She washed more blood off there. One thing she had to be thankful for, the bullet had gone straight through. It could have been a lot worse. Passing straight through his chest it had left a comparatively clean hole separating his ribs and grazing the sack of his left lung as near as she could judge. He was probably in great pain and would continue to be.

She fished the second cloth out of the steaming pot and, when it had sufficiently cooled, bathed the wound as well as she could. With the rest of the dry strips she bandaged it, rolling him from side to side as she worked. He did a lot of groaning and it hurt her to hear him but she knew it had to be done if she would keep down infection; and there was no guarantee that she could, even so. He had ought to be in bed.

She carried the water back out to the kitchen and poured it down the drain. Then she filled the pot with fresh water, poured in a little salt and put it back on the stove where she would have it handy.

She washed her hands again and went back and slumped down in a chair by the door. All the time she had worked with Cardigan she'd kept listening for the sound of approaching riders, and she was listening now.

After a while she got up and took off her dress in the bedroom and mended it. She put another dress on, a gay yellow-and-white print, in the hope it might serve to kind of buck up her spirits. Taking the rifle with her she went over to the cook shack and ate some cold beans which she found on the back of the gone-out stove. Then she went back to Cardigan.

He was moaning again but his eyes were open.

They considered each other for a bit without speaking. There was a kind of grudging admiration at the back of his eyes, but he didn't put any of it into his words. "In that letter you wrote you didn't mention Dodge City." The way he said it sounded like he was accusing her of something.

She said: "I don't recall that you mentioned being a horse thief, either."

"What's my politics got t' do with it? You claimed you was wantin' to tie up with a rancher—that you wanted some feller livin' west of the Pecos. That's me on both counts."

She let that go. "Can you get up if I help you?"

"I'll git up when I'm ready an' I don't need no help."

She lifted her chin and looked him straight in the eye. "You better get up now then. You ought to be in a bed."

She could see the bright anger boil into his stare. She had a temper herself and she put the whole business right square on the line. "I'm not one of your punchers. If we go on with this thing I'll expect to be treated as a wife and a partner. If I don't measure up to what you were looking for you can say so right now and I'll go on back to town."

The look of his eyes was like the smash of a hammer. "Back to that pianner-thumpin' tinhorn, I reckon!"

He climbed onto his feet then and stood towering over her with all the wild fury of a goaded bull. "If you're stayin' round here there's somethin' you better git straight right now. I don't want no pardner an' I ain't about t' hev one! Bein' a woman's your job an' what goes on outside of these rooms don't concern you. I told you straight out when I sent you that money—"

"I know what you told me. '*I ain't aimin' to buy no pig in a poke. I ain't reckonin' to be under no obligation till—*' "

"Correct," Cardigan scowled.

"All right. I'm here. You've looked me over. Now get into that bed before you're down with a—"

"Hold your lip," he glared, "till I git done with my talkin'. You'll git plain grub here an' plain talk an' no fripperies. I'll put food in your belly an' clothes on your back, but I'll run this spread any damn way I feel like an' I don't want no jawin' outa you about it, neither."

"Are you through?"

"No, I'm not through!" He seemed angered to hear his own voice going up while she stood there so cool, giving him back look for look. "You better know what you're gittin' into. I don't trim my lampwick fer no one. There's tough sleddin' ahead an', come I find that it's needful you'll do a

man's work same as everyone else. I ain't runnin' no rest
home—"

"I didn't ask for any rest home."

"You ain't gettin' one, neither! This ain't no country fer
weaklin's. You'll tend to the fire wood an' cook fer the outfit
such times as they're here, an' such times as they ain't you'll
take care of all stock that's bein' kept round the yard. You'll
turn your hand to whatever needs doin' an' you'll pleasure
my bed whenever it suits me."

She said with plain scorn: "What you want is a squaw."

The words didn't shame him, didn't bother him at all. She
was not quite certain of the way he looked at her; he appeared to be watching her. Almost, he appeared to be waiting.
It came over her suddenly what he had in his mind, and she
laughed to herself to see the way his face changed when she
said, quiet and scornful, "Though I suppose I could learn to
be one if had to."

The chagrin that darkened his eyes proved her right. His
talk had been designed to scare her off, to get rid of her; to
turn her away from here without delay.

She did not seek just then to uncover his reason; she was
much too engrossed with the discovery she had made—that
there was a lot more to Cardigan than showed on the surface.
Oh, he was dangerous, all right, a rough man and a tough
one, but not nearly so tough as he would have people think.
He could have told her straight out that he had had a change
of heart; instead he had resorted to subterfuge, had tried to
paint so dismal a picture that she would withdraw from their
arrangement of her own accord.

So there was softness in him, white mixed with the black.
Good hidden back of that hard blasphemous bluster. A kind
of modern Robin Hood with a code that would not let him
shoot an unarmed man.

She felt considerably better about her prospects for the
future.

She found he was still looking at her, obviously disgruntled.
"You mean you're figurin' t' stay here?"

"And where else would I go?"

There was no doubt but that he found her decision disturbing. Plainly he had counted on her going back to town. He seemed to want to speak out, to reveal some further disadvantage; and a perverse humor suddenly prompted her to say:

"You wanted a woman, so you sent me the price of my transportation. You weren't expecting too much for you didn't even bother to ask me for a picture. You couldn't believe your luck; the moment you laid eyes on me you made up your mind there was something rotten somewhere. You couldn't forget you'd found me being pawed by Frayne; your suspicions were confirmed when he told you he had known me in Dodge City."

Some memory darkened the look of her eyes. "Does every woman in Dodge City have to be a harlot? You don't even ask me *if* I were there, or what brought me there or what I was doing! You've heard I came out here with Top Hat Charlie and so, because he deals faro at the Gold Plate Saloon, you—"

"What *were* you doin' there?" Cardigan growled.

"I was with a variety show from St. Louis. I don't say Frayne didn't see me there—a lot of people saw me that I wouldn't know from Adam. But he had no right to say that he had 'known' me. No man can say that."

There was color in her cheeks when she finished, but it was the color of embarrassment and not of shame.

It would have been nice in him to have said he believed her, but he didn't say anything. Nor did he appear much impressed.

He unbuckled his cartridge belt and dropped it over the back of a chair. He shoved the door shut and dropped the bar into place.

"A hoofer, eh?"

Docie bridled. "If you think—"

"My head ain't workin' too good right now. I'm goin' t' catch a few winks," he said wearily, and grimaced. He licked at his lips and she suddenly realized how haggard his face looked. He took a long breath and let it slide out of him. "When the crew comes in wake me up," he grunted.

Then he paused and looked back at her. "You were right about one thing." A twisted grin lit up his tough face briefly. "You're a choicer piece of baggage than I'd any right t' look for."

When Hennessy, Cardigan's cook, quit the ranch he had his meagre belongings stuffed into the bedroll lashed back of his cantle and no least intention of ever coming back. Enough was enough and if, on top of everything else, Shiloh Frayne had no better sense than to start horsing round with that black-haired filly, it was time for a smart gent to roll his cotton.

He'd about made up his mind to do it anyway. Things was moving a sight too fast for any stove-up man who craved to keep on living. It was one thing to rustle maverick horses up north and something else again to start stealing from your neighbors. He'd seen some of those horses from Amado and Florence and the worked-over brands wasn't even healed yet! Lahr had claimed this new stealing was by Kurt's orders, and maybe it was; but that didn't take the damfool craziness out of it.

Nor out of setting in a deal where the deck was being stacked by any jasper like Lahr. You might's well ask for a rope and be done with it. People was getting fed up with this night riding and blood would be spilled in mighty grim earnest if it ever leaked out the KC was mixed up in it—they was plenty suspicious of the outfit already.

He'd been a fool ever to listen to Lahr in the first place. If Lahr would doublecross Cardigan he would doublecross anyone—Hennessy included.

With cold sweat on his neck he lifted his horse into a lope. He drew the carbine from its scabbard and rode with it cradled across the pommel of his saddle with his eyes jabbing this way and that through the shadows. He should have shaken the dust of this country right after Lahr put the deal up to him.

It had looked pretty slick the way Lahr had first told it.

A cinch, Lahr had said. Just as easy as knocking off skunks with a club.

There'd be just him and Hennessy; with the ranch for a stake and whatever they grabbed from the bank jobs. Not a chance for a slip-up—he'd got it all figured out. Alibis and everything. There was an old hat of Cardigan's hanging in the cook shack, and that's what they'd use to pin the whole thing on Kurt. They might look a little simple being tied in with a bunch of damn outlaws like that, and some folks might even make a few ugly cracks; but they could never prove anything. Not the way Lahr would play it.

He had it all fixed up. Stapleton, that owned the Gold Plate Saloon in Tucson, had been mixed up in some crooked deal Lahr had found out about, and that was the wedge he aimed to use for their alibi. Him and Hennessy only. Just the two of them. Clean as a fresh diaper.

Lahr would fix it for the bunch to rendezvous down at Frenchy's, a hole-up they knew about just east of Naco. It would take them a while to drift down there. Each man to ride separate so as not to attract any suspicious attention. Meantime Lahr, with Hennessy, and unbeknownst to the others, would ride in to Tucson and make themselves conspicuous in the Gold Plate Saloon where they'd proceed to tank up and, presumably, get plastered. Stapleton, ostensibly to forestall trouble, would publicly have words with them and apparently persuade them to take their arguments and their liquor into the privacy of the Gold Plate's back room. Where they would proceed to go on a three-day bender—according to Stapleton.

There were no windows opening off that back room and the only door was the one they'd go in by. Once they had shut it and locked it, however Stapleton—in the room above it—would lift an already-loosened plank from the wooden ceiling, let down a rope and haul them up. After which, from this upstairs room's window, with the same rope he'd let them down into the alley. And he'd take care of the appearances after they'd gone.

Rejoining the others at Frenchy's by a relay of horses they

would crack the Douglas bank the following night. Lahr
would be wearing Kurt's old hat and would manage to lose it
during the Copper State holdup at Bisbee. This, once the hat
was traced back to its owner, would pin the whole thing right
on Cardigan. Of course, Jupe Krailor and Frayne would be in
for it, too, but with their Gold Plate alibi Hennessy and Lahr
would be strictly in the clear. And Lahr already had a bill of
sale with Cardigan's signature faked slick as anything.

This was the way Lahr had put it up to him that hot afternoon while he'd been peeling potatoes; and the deal, so far,
had gone just like clockwork. The Douglas bank was just like
gutting a slut and that stage they'd stuck up hadn't fanched
them none, either. It was the butchery at Bisbee that had up-
set the applecart and first shown Hennessy what kind of a
bastard he had gone and tied up with. There had been no
need of Lahr killing that star-packer. It still sent cold chills all
through Hennessy's marrow to remember Lahr pumping slugs
into the lawman.

"Hell, I had t' make sure they'd get to work on that hat,"
Lahr said callously. "We can't grab the ranch until we git rid
of Cardigan."

Hennessy groaned as he flogged through the shadow-dap-
pled moonlight night. He'd been a fool to get mixed up in this
thing. Any guy as slick as Lahr was at fixing things up wouldn't
find no trouble getting rid of a partner.

The best thing now, Hennessy told himself, was to head
straight south and get on over into Mexico. And he was there
in his thinking, bemoaning the follies of a misspent life, when
something jerked tight about his arms and chest and dragged
him headlong from the saddle.

Roped!

The truth raced like fire across the havoc of his thoughts.
And then the whole world exploded in a million glittering
lights.

The next thing he knew a rough hand had hold of him and
he felt himself being hauled to his feet. Then his head cleared
a little and he mighty near fainted when he found himself
peering into the face of Curly Lahr.

Lahr's expression was not pleasant.

Hennessy swallowed twice and shuddered.

Jupe Krailor held the end of the rope with his weight on his boot heels thirty feet away.

Hennessy gagged and Lahr said thinly: "Where the hell did you figure to be goin' in such a lather?"

There it was. Right there was the crux of this whole situation.

Terror broke Hennessy's brain from its paralysis. His thoughts flew round like a fly in a bottle, but his tongue couldn't seem to get hold of any words.

"Well?" Lahr said, his tone sharp and vicious.

"I . . . uh . . . wasn't goin' anyplace, partic'lar."

Hennessy sweated.

"You allus go noplace in such a hell-tearin' hurry?"

"I was lookin' for you. There's a woman at the ranch; right young an' damn good lookin'. Says she's waitin' fer Cardigan."

"What kind of a yarn are you tryin' to patch up?"

"By Gawd, it's the truth! Someone fetched her out from town. She was there when I rode in—had her bag right on the doorstep. Wanted to know where Kurt was an' when I tells her he's pulled out she wasn't bothered even a little bit. Jest give me a grin. 'He's expecting me,' she says, an' takes her bag on into the house.

"Then Frayne comes ridin' in. I kept my mouth shut till we was plumb through eatin'. Then she put on a light an' of course I had t' tell him. He was hog-wild to go over. I done what I could an' when I seen he was goin' over anyway I piled into a saddle an' come huntin' you—an' I kin prove it. You kin see her for yourself jest as quick as we git back!"

Lahr eyed him for several moments, never saying a word. Then he signed Jupe Krailor to ease up on the rope and, when Jupe did, he loosened the loop and let Hennessy get out of it.

Hennessy plainly had the fidgets. "You're goin' back there, ain'tcha?"

Lahr tossed the loop to Krailor and grinned and shook his head.

"But— You know what Frayne'll do!"

"I ain't Frayne's keeper."

"But—"

"There's times I find it pretty good business to let nature take its course," Lahr said. "You can take the hulls off these nags, Jupe. We're goin' to stick right here a spell an' give Frayne's talent a chance to exercise."

Krailor guffawed. Hennessy looked worried. "What if—"

Lahr said, "That's why we're waitin'. Kurt'll be back if he told that filly t' meet him there. If he walks in on Frayne it's goin' to be too bad for someone. There's a fair-sized possibility it might be too bad for Kurt."

19

COMMON GROUND

Sam Sollantsy folded up the week-old copy of the Tombstone *Epitaph* and, with a snort of disgust, chucked it over with the others on the marshal's desk. He had been through them all and was no nearer solving the Douglas and Bisbee bank robberies than he'd been last night when Esparza had refused to go after Kurt Cardigan. The brief accounts in the *Star* and the rambling through colorful diatribes taking up half the pages of the Brewery Gulch *Gazette* only gave additional fuel to his contempt of local law.

"It's plain as the nose on your face," he said bitterly. "A kid in three-cornered pants could see the same damn bunch is pullin' all this stuff. Settin' on your tail ain't going to slice no pickles! Four men stick up the Tombstone stage; four men go larrupin' hell-for-leather out of Douglas right after the safe at the bank was blown; three men stick up the Copper State at Bisbee while a fourth waits outside with the horses. God a'mighty, what more do you want?"

"Proof of their identity," Esparza said quietly. "We have nothing but conjecture to connect the same four men with all three jobs and nothing but suspicion to hook them up with

Cardigan. I want facts, not surmise and suspicion. Show me one fact that ties Cardigan into this and I'll—"

"I've shown you three facts an' you won't act on any of them."

"You've said the yellow stud Cardigan rides is the Hale stallion, Jubal Jo, from Big Timber. You've said the buttermilk filly Cardigan bought for you at the livery is another Hale horse, and you've said Cardigan forced you out of town at gun point. But the livery keeper, Reagan, says he didn't buy the filly from Cardigan; he says he didn't see Cardigan throw a gun on you. And *I* didn't see him throw a gun on you and, for all you know, Kurt may have bought this Jubal Jo from somebody else—"

"Then why not go out there an' ask him? Make him produce a bill of sale. Make him round up the stock he's got out there an' let us look it over." The Tri-States man said bitterly: "You know damn well in your own mind that crowd's guilty!"

The marshal shook his head. "I think the KC crew may be implicated in some of this violence that's been going on, but thoughts are not proof. And we've nothing at all to connect them with those bank jobs. As a matter of record, and according to Stapleton and several others, at the time those banks were being robbed the KC cook and the KC range boss were having themselves a bender right here in town in the Gold Plate Saloon."

"Just because those two didn't happen to be in on it doesn't alibi the whole outfit, does it?" Sollantsy snorted. "The bulk of his gang may not work on the ranch, may not have no connection with the KC at all. If he's got any cogs in his noggin he'd have his bunch scattered out, one guy workin' here, another one there."

Esparza said, "There's no point goin' all over it again. You may be absolutely right in callin' Cardigan responsible for the stealin' in your country and the Tri-States crowd may have enough to convict him, but until it's put before me I'll consider this end first. I'm a lot more concerned with getting back that bank loot, and the men responsible for those killings at Bisbee, than I am with somethin' that happened somewhere else. And, since the fellow you're after happens to be the very man I'm dependin' on to help me get back the money that was stolen in those—"

"But it's the same goddam man!" Sollantsy shouted. "An' I'll be campin' right here until I take the bastard back with me!"

"That's your—" Esparza quit talking as a man in dusty range garb stepped through the door. He looked at the man carefully. "Glad you're back, Hankins. What'd you find out?"

The deputy tossed a hat to Esparza. It was old and sunfaded and grimed about the band with an ingrained coating of dust and sweat. "This hat was dropped by the leader of that bunch when they went poundin' away from the Copper State —the guy that cut down the Bisbee marshal. If you don't recognize it," Hankins said, "turn it over an' hev a look at the sweatband. Notice them initials? I just been talkin' to Kransfeldter down at the Mercantile. He stamped them initials in that hat for Kurt Cardigan."

Cardigan didn't sleep well. The pain in his chest was like a white-hot iron and its heat spread all through him. Awake he could fight back the pain, could clamp his jaws shut and ignore it, but in sleep it kept him twisting and groaning. Sometimes he was a luckless prospector caught by the Apaches and staked out on an ant hill; at other times he was afoot in the burning glare of the desert, trying to track down his burros with an empty canteen. But always, when the dreams or the pain finally woke him, the black haired girl was either close by or bending over him, wiping his face or putting cold rags against the heat in his forehead.

God, but he was hot!

The funny part of it was he didn't seem to get delirious. He always knew who she was and what she was doing there. Each time he woke up her face would bring it all back. He'd had a damn close call and he knew it. An inch either way and you could have what was left of him.

Sometimes he was awake when he'd make out like he was sleeping—playing possum, kind of, just to see what she'd be up

to, or to have himself a look when she bent over to put the
cloths on. She was a damn good looking baggage—best he'd
ever laid his eyes on; a cool hand, too, and gritty, he thought,
recalling the way she had fought against Frayne and the way
she'd faced up to him afterwards. Too bad this deal had got so
loused up. Mebbe, if things had been different . . .

He said one time: "You better git some sleep," but every
time he come to himself, there she was, still with him. Still
wringing out cloths or putting their dampness against his hot
face. She had the lamp turned way down and the shutters
barred over the window and his rifle propped ready not two
foot from her hand.

Practical. By God, you had to give her that much. Practical and pretty as a basket of chips.

He said, "Why don't you go an' git yourself some rest?"

"I'm doing all right. Besides, it's almost daylight. Do you
want me to fix you—"

"I don't seem t' feel like eatin'."

"I'll get you a drink," she said; and he heard her working
the skreaky pump in the kitchen. And then she was back with
a dipperful, holding his head up, and its smooth, soothing
freshness was cooling to his throat.

"Bleedin' stopped?" he asked as he sank back again.

She gave him a nod. "You don't get much with that kind
of wound; it had stopped when you got here." She took another rag from the pan she had handy. "How'd you happen
to get it?"

"Carelessness. Some guy took a shot at me out in the
brush."

Pain laid hold of him and tightened the line of his jaw for a
moment. She leaned impulsively forward. "I know it's bad,
Kurt. I wish I might bear some part of it for ycu. If you can
think of anything I *could* do . . ."

He shook his head and grimaced. And afterwards he looked
at her with a long, searching stare. There was a depth to this
girl, a steadiness and fortitude he had not previously noticed.
Looking at her this way made a man feel—But there was no

good in building pictures. Perhaps, if he had managed to
come across her sooner—

He said abruptly: "You'll find my horse around here some-
place. Big yellow stallion with a red mane an' tail—name's
Snuffy. Wisht you'd take an' pull the gear off him an' put him
in the corral so's he'll have a chance t' roll. You might throw
him a armful of hay while you're at it, an' get him a can of
oats from the bin in the barn. Uh . . ." He said, carefully picking his words, "You might do a sight better t' git on him an'
get outa here. There's more to this thing than you know about
an' it ain't goin' t' git no better."

The shadows of the room etched and clarified her features
and her eyes explored his face with a quiet yet quick attention. She laid another cool rag against his forehead and sat
back again, gently shaking her head. "I'll stick to my part of
the bargain, Kurt—"

"I made no bargain!" he reminded her sharply.

"I know." Her eyes looked black in this light. He had not
noticed before how they slanted at the corners or how her lips
revealed each shift of her thoughts. He watched them now,
how they parted and met again, full and red against the ivory
smoothness of her face. And he saw the black shine of her
hair while she held herself still, almost as though she were inviting this inspection.

And something robust and intense and unsettling ran between them; and he looked at her with a sultry thoroughness,
seeing how completely she was the end of every trail.

He swung his feet to the edge of the bed and sat up, still
eyeing her, as unconscious of pain as he was of the damp cloth
sliding off his forehead. He seemed completely engrossed and
they came to their feet as of one accord. Color showed and
fell out of her cheeks and her arms came up and crossed her
breasts; and then she let her hands fall to her sides and he
pulled her against him roughly and kissed her.

They came apart breathless and trembling and she watched
him with eyes that were wide and searching. She looked queer
standing there like that and just staring. He felt queer himself; nothing like such a feeling had ever got into him.

He reached for her again but she stepped back away from him.

"No, Kurt . . . not yet." There was something high and proud and shining in her eyes; and he said, "Docie!" and started toward her again.

But she cried: "Wait—" and stopped, as though she would offer some further explanation. He saw it fade out of her and saw the quick rise and fall of her breathing, and was profoundly disturbed.

He took a deep breath; and she said, "After we're married—"

His harsh laugh stopped her. "What give you that idea?"

"But you said . . ."

"I said what you could expect if you stayed here—I didn't say nothin' about gettin' hitched up. A variety show hoofer ain't my idea of wife material."

20

"AND TAKE THAT CARRION WITH YOU!"

*H*E DREAMED he was lost in the desert. That he'd been wandering for hours in that trackless waste trying to reach a shimmering lake of water; but every time he got to where he thought the lake was, there was no water there, just the blistering sands. Again and again he clawed to his feet and went staggering on; and always, ahead of him like a will-o'-the-wisp, was the beckoning gleam of that tranquil lake with the white gulls wheeling and flashing above it. So real it looked—so cool and blue! And then he saw the tall shape of a comely woman. Young and handsome, she was, and coming toward him with the black hair flying round her face like a veil. And then her red lips parted and he recognized Docie. "Come," she said, "and I will show you the way."

And then someone was shaking him violently; and he came

out of the dream with a cold sweat on him to find Docie bending over him.

"There are riders coming into the yard," she said quickly,
and he was awake on the instant.

He saw the sun's yellow pattern of brightness on the floor
and knew he had slept a lot longer than he'd aimed to. He
swung his feet off the bed and she handed him the dipper. He
threw her a slanchways look at he emptied it.

There was no sign of tears and she met his glance coolly.

He set the dipper on the bed. "Get me a shirt—in that chest
over there. I don't want them bastards t' know I been
wounded."

From the drawers she said, "There's nothing here but this
pink thing—"

"What's the matter with that?" He growled: "Fetch it here."

She handed it to him and then brought his gun belt and
watched while he strapped it about his lean hips; watched
him dig out his pistol from under the pillow. "You ought to
stay in that bed."

He flipped open the cylinder, making sure it was loaded,
and swapped one cartridge for another from his belt. Then he
tucked in his shirt and slipped the gun's barrel between the
shirt and his pants; it was only then that she noticed his belt
had no holster.

He tossed her another of those close, searching glances. "So
you made up your mind to be the dog at my table."

She bit her lip, but she was not the kind to cry or dodge
round a thing. She met his eyes straightly. Flat and level, she
said: "I haven't decided what I will do." Her voice faded
down to a throaty whisper. "I hadn't expected to fall in
love . . ."

He looked at her sharply and stopped in his tracks. For the
space of three heartbeats he stood entirely still, considering
her with his completest attention.

The sound of talk drifted in from the yard; horse sound, too,
and the tiny melody of a tinkling spur chain; but Cardigan's
eyes never left the girl's face.

There was incredulity in the way he regarded her, and outrage, despair and, beyond these things, a startled and brightening gleam of real pleasure which he could not quite hide.

He reached out and took hold of her shoulders, and the hope was still there and the doubt and uncertainty. "You mean . . . with *me?*"

She said with her lips pulled back from her teeth: "Do you imagine yourself the only man in this country?"

One moment longer he stared at her, then he clamped his jaws shut and wheeled out of the room.

Jupe Krailor was stripping the gear from the horses when Cardigan opened the door and stepped out. Hennessy's look was plainly uneasy but a wry grin twisted Lahr's florid face and he put up a hand and said, "Glad you're back."

"Didn't you reckon I'd be?"

Lahr ignored the black truculence in Cardigan's voice and said, "Sure—but ten days is ten days an' we was beginnin' t' git worried. Thought mebbe you'd run into trouble or somethin'—"

"Wouldn't of figured you had much time to be worried with all of the runnin' around you been doin'. What have you done with that stock you been grabbin'?"

Lahr's green eyes shifted warily. "What stock is that?"

"All them horses you run off from Chandler, Amado, Cortaro an' Florence."

"Why," said Lahr easily, "we've scattered 'em round the place like we always do—"

"Who you been workin' for, yourself or Esparza?"

Lahr must have felt the startled looks of the other two for he stood with a visible strain on his features. Then he laughed, over loud, and said, "Hell, fer a minute I thought you was serious."

"You thought right," Cardigan said: "an' you ain't answered the question."

"What the hell you gettin' at? All we been doin' is follerin' your orders—"

"That's a goddam lie an' you know it!"

Lahr's green eyes narrowed. "Be a little careful with that kinda talk. Them's fightin' words—"

"I'll repeat 'em if you want. I've never run off a branded horse in my life, or ordered one run off, or stole off my neighbors—an' you damn well know it."

Lahr's brick-red skin was tight as a drumhead across the jut of his cheekbones. He said to the others with a lean, hateful smile, "You see how it is? He's got a woman here now an' he wants t' git shut of us. Any excuse'll do when a man gits a hankerin'—"

"You doublecrossin' dog!"

Lahr put on the look of a martyr. "So I'm a doublecrosser now. You lay out the orders an' I shove 'em through, an' then you get a woman an' a new set of notions an' that makes me a doublecrossin' dog. I guess you'll try t' say next you never even told me to stick up them banks—"

"I'll tell you somethin' right now!" Cardigan snarled, striding toward him. "Gather up your stole horses an' git offa this ranch—the whole pack an' passel of you!"

But Lahr stood his ground. Malevolence flashed in the look he gave Kurt. "You heard the boss, boys. He don't need us no more so he's throwin' us out. Us that's built up this place for him, livin' in the leather for weeks at a time, takin' his orders an' riskin' our necks like a bunch of pelados so he can play the fine gentleman an' be known all over as the biggest horse breeder in five hundred miles. Don't stand there like fools—take off your hats to him! Ain't he known all up an' down the Spanish Trail for the quality of the stock we've run his brand on?

"We better pack up our duds an' git goin', I reckon, 'fore he gets around t' siccin' that marshal on us. We ain't good enough for him now he's turnin' respectable on the money you an' me put into his pockets."

Lame Hennessy scowled. Krailor licked at his lips and dropped a hand toward his belt gun.

Cardigan never took his eyes off Lahr. His face was black as the wrath of God. And each grim stride fetched him nearer the range boss.

A slow wind lifted the flaps of Lahr's vest. Some dark remembrance thinned his lips and his upper body tipped a little forward, settling his weight on the balls of his feet. But the look of his eyes did not back up that pose and Hennessy stepped back away from him quickly; and Lahr cried out: "Stop right there—stop it, Kurt!"

But Cardigan kept coming, slow stride by stride, inexorably nearer, the steady crunch of his boots the only sound in that stillness.

Lahr's eyes sprang wide and grew bright with panic. He went back half a step, but it wasn't far enough. He threw up both arms but they weren't enough, either. Cardigan's rock-hard right ripped through that defense and smashed him full in the mouth.

Lahr's head rocked back. His eyes rolled wildly. He bared his teeth and spat out two broken ones and Cardigan's left fist flattened his nose.

The range boss loosed a great yell and, beyond thinking now, made a frantic and desperate grab for his gun.

Like a pile-driver, Cardigan's right struck Lahr's belly.

At that time, exactly, Docie came to the door. She heard the agonized outrush of Lahr's expelled breath, saw him fold and go crazy-like round in a circle with his chin on his knees and an animal whimper dribbling out of his throat. Then his knees let go and he pitched face down in the hoof-tracked dust and lay there writhing like a snake with its back broke.

She heard Cardigan then, the wheezy rasp of his breathing, and caught the white look of his twisted cheeks. He stood wholly alone out there in the open with his big hands still fisted and the look of his eyes holding Krailor and the cook grayly frozen in their tracks. She was reminded of a huge and battered grizzly at bay; there was no give-up in him, no consciousness of odds.

She found it hard to untangle the effect it had on her, seeing him standing out there like that. The pain of his wound must be setting him crazy; yet nothing but a dark and blazing fury looked out of him as he stood there waiting for whatever the others would do.

Both men were watching him closely and both kept their hands well away from their pistols. There was a strange, puzzled look in Jupe Krailor's stare as though he could not believe what he had just seen happen. Hennessy's look was an expression of pure fright.

Cardigan's lips flattened out and thinly showed the white of his teeth, and the wind that ran whispering through the overhead branches ruffled the yellow hair at his temples and molded the sleeves against the muscles of his arms.

Hennessy's cheeks had turned gray as wood ash and, under that prolonged scrutiny, even Jupe Krailor began to show his disquiet.

Lahr groaned and stirred. With both hands in the dust he came onto a knee. He groaned again and looked stupidly around him. And then he got to his feet and his eyes found Cardigan and turned brightly wicked.

"Got enough?" Cardigan said.

The range boss weaved away a few steps and drew a hand across his mouth and wiped the hand on his trousers.

"Get his horse for him, Krailor."

Lahr looked up with a scowl. "You're feelin' mighty proud, but don't overdo it."

Cardigan said to Krailor: "Put the saddles on all three of them"; and Hennessy took the first full breath since he had come here.

Behind the blood and dust ground into them Lahr's roan cheeks turned suddenly bitter. "What about that money we banked with you—the money for that stuff we got up north?"

"It's goin' back to the men who lost those horses."

"Do you think I'll let you get away with that?"

Cardigan's mouth showed a meager smile; it was all the answer he bothered to give and there was no smile in his eyes at all. Krailor came up with their mounts and Lahr reached for his reins in a shaking fury.

"You ain't done with this—"

"Go on—go on," Cardigan said. "Get out of here."

It was then, while Kurt had his back to her, watching them, that Docie heard the rasp of some sound and stared, cold with horror, as Shiloh Frayne came around the corner of the house behind Cardigan, immediately throwing the rifle to his shoulder.

But the sound of that movement, or the bright wink of metal, warned Cardigan. He dropped flat and whirled as the crash of Frayne's shot clouted the fronts of the buildings. He rose up on one knee and flame licked from his pistol. The rifle fell out of Frayne's loosening grasp and he spun half around and collapsed, choking, sideways.

Lahr snatched a dropped hand clear away from his gun butt and threw both hands high over his head as Cardigan's glance swept around with his pistol. And then Kurt got up.

"Now get out," he said bitterly—"and take that carrion with you!"

21

THE FINGER WRITES

T HERE IS always a certain excitement attendant to any kind of chase or hunt. When the hunt happens to have a man as the recipient of its interest the concomitant furor customarily mounts in direct proportion to that man's importance, position or the number of dollars which have been offered for his capture. When Sam Sollantsy let it be known that Frank Esparza was gathering a posse to go after Kurt Cardigan the excitement became terrific.

The news spread like wildfire. All over town men suspended their regular employment to speak of it; the cobbler quit his last to run out into the street, knife in hand, and shout the tidings to the Mexican barber; the barber left a customer half shaved and dashed off with his razor to impart the news to the Italian butcher; the butcher dropped his cleaver, wiped his hands on his apron and went to the nearest saloon with the tale; half the men at the bar rushed off with the story and one of them took it to Big Tooth Emma who told her girls who told their customers who promptly purveyed it all over town. And, after the manner of stories, the news lost little through these many retellings.

Inside a half hour there were half a hundred versions being circulated with gusto. Cardigan was exposed as the chief of the horse-stealing gang which had been harrying ranchers all over the Southwest. He was king of the gang which had been robbing the stages. He had 'blown' the Douglas Bank several nights ago and, with ten masked Yaquis from below the border, had stuck up the Copper State in broad daylight, killing the Bisbee marshal and the agent at Butterfield's Bisbee station. He had raped a nester girl north of town. With a gang of forty tough night-riding rustlers he was trying to take over the entire Territory and turn it into an outlaw's paradise with himself as overlord. . . .

Whatever you wanted to hear, you could hear it. He was an escaped lifer from Yuma. He was Curly Bill. He was one of the James boys. He was one of the gang who'd been riding with Bonney who was being driven out of New Mexico and aimed to set up headquarters at Tucson. He was the right-hand man of Billy the Kid. He was a cousin of Chisum, the cattle king. . . .

Everyone was going to join the posse. Everyone wanted a crack at this killer who was turning the Territory into a shambles. Killed four men at Amado—a dozen more around Florence. He had sixteen notches on his gun right now and swore he wouldn't quit till he had a round two dozen. . . .

Talk was cheap and, as usual, noisy; but it took a bit of intestinal fortitude or a good private reason to have your name bruited round as being connected with a posse sworn to bring in a man as expert with a gun as Kurt Cardigan. Hard as Sollantsy worked—and he was indefatigable—it was nightfall before Esparza's posse was ready to take to the field.

It numbered nine men, including Esparza and Sollantsy, when it left the marshal's office at 9:00 p.m. Sollantsy had rounded up about as many more but Esparza had refused to swear them in on the contention that justice would be poorly served by men of debatable character. The rejects were drifters and barroom bums. Sollantsy was not too disgruntled; he had spent the intervening time since his arrival in pinning down an abundance of local gossip and felt reasonably confident that most of the men sworn in would do their best to fix Cardigan's clock.

There was himself and Esparza. There was the Flowerpot owner and his foreman, Zeke Smith, who had no more reason to be tender about Cardigan than had Joe Nettleton of the Straddle-Bug, an outfit which had also lost heavily to horse thieves. There was Esparza's deputy, Hankins, who had fetched Cardigan's hat back from Bisbee. There was Ed Reagan, the livery stable proprietor, who may or may not have purchased stolen stock from Cardigan. There was Tom Steins, the local gunsmith and finally, loudly sponsored by Sollantsy, there was the piano-playing gambler, Top Hat Charlie.

Five miles out of town these watchdogs of the law were joined by the nester, Rickven, who vociferously held Kurt Cardigan responsible for the present unwonted condition of his daughter and who declared, with some justice, that no one in the posse knew Cardigan's layout and the adjacent country as thoroughly as he did. After considerable argument Sollantsy prevailed upon Esparza to include him.

Before they'd left town Esparza had routed out two other men for posse work, a man named Hazelton and Farquas Torney. Hazelton was an up-country rancher for whom Kurt had worked when he'd first come into the country. Torney was a blacksmith from up around Oracle whose young son Cardigan once had rescued from a runaway horse. Both were favorably disposed toward Cardigan and Sollantsy had howled about "prejudice" until Esparza had crossed them off the list. The way the deal stacked up now, the Tri-States man felt pretty well convinced that justice would be done without a lot of red tape.

After the departing KC crew had reached a point some half mile or so from Cardigan's headquarters, Lahr flung a hand up and called for a halt. "Go up ahead a piece, Jupe," he told

Krailor, "an' keep your eyes peeled while Hennessy an' me git rid of Frayne's body."

When Krailor was out of earshot, Hennessy said, "What's—"

But Lahr cut him off. "This'll work out better than the way we had it figured. That bastard dealt us the ace of spades when he put that slug through Frayne an' made us pack ol' Shiloh out of there. I been doin' a little thinkin' an' we really got him now."

There was a smug satisfaction about his look as he hooked a knee round the horn of his saddle and, digging out the makings, started rolling up a smoke. "Here's the way it stacks up. Two months ago Kurt sold me the place, but there was a clause in the deal that I wasn't to get possession till he'd got all his stock moved off the KC range. In the meantime, you come to me with a hint that you figured Kurt was crooked— that you'd noticed a couple horses with some damn peculiar brands. You got that?"

Hennessy nodded.

"All right, then. We decided to look around an' see what Cardigan was up to. He had always seemed like a pretty good guy an' had always seemed to be squarely on the level; but them two horses had got us t' thinkin'. We begun to watch Cardigan; we found he was doin' a heap of night ridin'. Every few nights he'd slip off from the ranch; sometimes we'd find out in time t' take after him but, until last night, he'd always give us the slip. Last night we was ready for him. We had let Frayne in on it an' he was with us. We trailed Kurt up t' that draw near Black Mountain. There was a shack up there an' a bunch of horses tied round to the back. We left ours in the brush an' injuned up there an' me—I got a look in at the winder. There was Cardigan an' three-four other guys splittin' up the cash from them bank jobs.

"You come up then an' had a look, too. You heard Cardigan say t' some beetle-browed gent with chin whiskers that the game around here was about played out an' that it might be smart to clear out of these parts. The beetle-browed guy says it would of been all right if Cardigan hadn't gunned the Bisbee marshal. Then a consumptive-lookin' jasper with a limp

wants t' know what they're figurin' t' do about the horses, an'
Cardigan says they can be sold just as good over around Ajo
an' that might be a pretty good place t' work out of. Beetle-
brow wants t' know when Kurt figures t' leave here, an' Kurt
says they'll pull out the day after t'morrow.

"We don't wait for no more but light a shuck out of there.
We spend the rest of the night ridin' the KC range an' what
we find is a bunch of stock wearin' fresh-altered brands in a
little hole up near the Ironwood Seep. Looks to us like this is
some of that stuff that was run off from Florence an' Amado.

"We're struck pretty hard, findin' out what a skunk Kurt
has turned out t' be. We'd always figured he was straight—
never had no cause t' think otherwise; an' prob'ly, if you hadn't
spotted them two horses the other day he'd of got clean away
with it an' skipped the country. But now we understand a
whole pile of queer things which we hadn't never give much
thought to before—like Kurt bein' off on so many trips an' all,
which we'd figured he was just off buyin' an' sellin' horses."

Hennessy said: "What about the girl?"

Lahr scowled a moment, then he shook his head. "She
don't make no difference. It was close to eleven when Cardigan got home—she can't prove where he was before he got
here."

"She kin prove where Frayne was."

"All right. We leave Frayne out of it. You an' me follered
Cardigan. You an' me rode the range an' found the stole
horses. This mornin' we told Frayne. This afternoon the three
of us rode in an' Frayne pops it at him. Frayne says: 'What
do you know about that bunch of stole horses we found—'
That's as far as he gits when Kurt grabs his gun an' goes t'
smokin'. We was still on our horses. Frayne manages t' stick
in his saddle till we git outa range. Meantime his horse goes
lame. We turn the horse loose, knowin' we got t' git Frayne
to town quick or he'll cash in. I take him up on my horse but
he passes out anyway before we can get there—an' here, by
Gawd, is his body t' prove it!" Lahr grinned at the cook. "An'
what's wrong with that?"

"Esparza will wanta know where you got the money t' buy Cardigan's ranch—"

"Hell, my uncle in Kokomo left it to me in his will."

"Well, but . . ." Hennessy hesitated. "What about the girl?"

"It's just her word ag'in ours. They got nothin' against us. We got a castiron alibi for the time of them bank robbin's."

Hennessy ran nervous fingers around the inside of his collar. "I got a feelin'—"

"Hell, you always got a feelin'." Lahr pitched his smoke away and shoved his boot back into the stirrup. "Look, there ain't no sense us leavin' empty-handed. Once we've told Frank Esparza our story he will surer'n hell bring a posse out here an' they'll clean this range of everything we got on it. We might's well gather up a little of the cream—wouldn't take us more'n a little while t' shove twenty or thirty head of the best down into them river bottoms south of the mission. Frayne'll keep limber f'r another five-six hours. We could leave 'im right here an'—"

"What about Jupe? Where you fittin' him in?"

"Yeah," Lahr said, "Jupe Krailor. That's right. He ain't the kind a man could put much trust in. Kinda weak in the head. No tellin' what he'd do—liable t' open his mouth an' put his foot right in it . . . I guess," he said at last, "we better salt Jupe down. We'll let him help us with them horses . . ."

Night had long since rolled the range up in its blanket. Docie, after the departure of the sacked KC crew, had seen Kurt back into bed, had caught a few hours' sleep and then had got up and fixed herself a little supper from the ample supplies she had found in the cook shack. She had changed her dress.

She had looked in on Kurt and given him some more water. She didn't know when he'd last eaten but she didn't dare give him any solids with that fever. His bout with Curly Lahr had fetched it way up again and she could hear him in there now, twisting and groaning in his sleep; but there was nothing she could do for him she hadn't already done. There was no good fooling with that hole in his chest. It was up to God what happened to him now.

He was tough as an ox. She had never seen a man with as much vitality. Yet if that wound became infected. . . .

She pulled her thoughts away from that.

She tried to consider what she herself had ought to do, but she gave that up, too. Somehow it didn't seem to matter. In the vast reach of this country, this monstrous hush and desolation, the acts of any one man or woman appeared trivial and commonplace, almost without significance. She was astonished she could think of herself in that fashion.

She watched the moon come up, round and red, behind the rugged outline of blue-black mountains and felt the welcome coolness of a breeze rising off the desert. She couldn't see it but knew it was down there below her, mile on tawny mile of it, brooding, waiting, patient as the eternal slopes that ringed it.

She had no conception of passing time. Of what account was time in a land so vast? The mystic radiance of the risen moon was now all about her, silvering the yonder ridgetops and spreading before her incredulous gaze a whole new world of ethereal beauty. A great peace stole over her and she listened to the run of the wind in the branch tops. She let the rifle rest in her lap and settled back comfortably against the doorframe. The last thing she heard was the stomp of a hoof in Snuffy's corral.

She must have slept.

The next thing she knew she was sitting bolt upright, the rifle clutched in her hands, listening into the wind-riven night. She could not guess what had wakened her. The yard was filled with the movement of shadows and she heard the wind tearing through the cottonwoods; and fear pressed cold fingers against her heart.

She got up thinking Kurt, while she slept, might have called her. Her frightened glance raced round the yard. Nothing moved there. The shapes were just shadows. Faintly, faroff, through the rush of the wind, she could hear the ululating cry of a coyote, and then a spatter of sounds that might have been shots—that *were* shots; suddenly she knew it.

In the corral Snuffy nickered and flung up his head.

There was a rumble of hoofs in the teeth of the wind, now loud, now soft, but at each loudening nearer. The wind flapped her skirt and fear closed round her heart with the stark omniscient grip of foreboding. She whirled and ran through the house to rouse Kurt.

But he was already up and pulling on his spurred boots. He stamped his heels into them and reached for his gun.

"What is it?" she cried.

He shook his head grimly. "You should of gone while you could—you're trapped into this now." He scowled as he buckled his shell belt around him. He sloshed on his hat and caught up the rifle. "Git into a pair of my pants an' come into the yard just as quick as you're ready."

He swung on his heel and went hurrying doorward.

She had boots in her bag; they'd been a part of her act—boots and a hat and a red bandanna. While she kicked off her pumps and got into the boots, wind fetched her the pound of those oncoming ponies and she ran to the door, stood there breathless and staring.

Cloud half covered the face of the moon. In the corral Snuffy blew out a gusty breath and his shrill, whistling challenge rang over the yard.

Out yonder was tumult, a gray blur of movement. Horses tore through the brush by the gate and came thundering past with dilated nostrils, and a second wave of shapes knifed through the dark trees and the clatter of slithering hoofs was all around her.

Three hatted heads showed against the white clouds and the moon came out and she saw these men's faces—the faces of the crew Kurt Cardigan had fired!

22

A NIGHT IN THE HILLS

*C*URLY LAHR stopped his horse within ten feet of her, a high black shape against the sky, as Cardigan came up with the yellow stud.

"Didn't I tell you, Lahr, to git off this ranch?"

"Well, Jesis Christ, we been *tryin'* t' git off it! We started roundin' up them horses like you told us t' do—had 'em all bunched an' strung out for the border. Comin' onto the Tanque Verde flats we run smack into a goddam posse an' that loco fool, Krailor, opened up with a rifle! Knocked Zeke Smith off his horse first crack—"

"What'd you *want* me t' do—git hung fer a hossthief?"

"This ain't no time fer jawin'," Hennessy growled. "That bunch'll be onto us if we don't git outa here."

"How many was they?"

"Hell's fire," Krailor snarled—"must be fifteen-twenty of 'em. They was spread all over the goddam flats."

Cardigan said: "We'll head for Mammoth. They can't track us in the dark an'—" He swung a look toward the house and saw Docie. "What the hell are you waitin' for? Thought I told you—"

Docie's chin came up. "I'm not one of your dogs."

Even in the moonlight he could see her eyes flash, could catch the hostile tone of her. Then contempt edged her voice and something else came into it. "You're a fool if you go with them. You fired these men and their troubles with the law are no concern of yours."

Lahr laughed harshly.

Docie kept her eyes on Cardigan. "Listen to me, Kurt. Don't throw your life away. I heard you fire these men this afternoon for stealing horses. I'll tell the sheriff—"

"You wouldn't get the chance," Kurt said. "Any talkin' they

do'll be done with rifles. Some them moguls round Tucson have been layin' for me. I'd be shot deader'n hell 'fore you could open your mouth. Now get into them pants."

Docie stood her ground. "If you go with these men you can't ever come back here; when you run from the law you have to keep on running—"

"For Chri'sake," Hennessy snarled. "How long you goin' t' jaw with that woman?"

And Krailor said: "Listen!"

Down the wind came the thunder of hard-running horses, still faint and far, but getting louder every moment.

"Get into them pants!" Cardigan told her.

"I'll go with you on just one condition—"

"You'll go with me an' like it, just the way you are. You had your chance t' pull outa this—a sight better chance'n *I* ever had."

Hennessy cursed. "You goin' t' gab all night?"

The sound of the posse was drawn immeasurably nearer. Even Krailor showed tension in the spasmodic way he kept roweling his pony.

"Jupe," Cardigan growled, "find Miz Balinett a horse."

"I won't go," Docie said; but Cardigan was onto her before she could slam the door. She struck at him with her fists and he slapped her across the face with an oath. He caught her behind the knees with one arm and scooped her, kicking, up onto his shoulder.

"You can take Jupe up behind you," he told Hennessy, and dumped her, still kicking, into Krailor's saddle. In the moonlight her pantalets looked like white trousers and he grinned at her futile attempts to hold her dress down. "I told you t' wear pants."

Krailor came up. "I can't find her no—Hell's bells! She can't hev *my* hoss!"

"Climb up behind Hennessy," Kurt said unfeelingly, and to Docie: "You gonna behave or do I got t' tie you on there?"

He didn't wait for an answer. He took Krailor's rifle; shoved it into the man's hands. "Git up behind Hennessy." He took

Docie's reins and strode over to the dun and swung into the saddle.

Sound of the posse's oncoming horses seemed ominously close but if Cardigan noticed it seemed not to bother him. "Swing left of the house an' go through the back pasture. House'll keep 'em from seein' us till we've got out of rifle range. They'll waste a little time tryin' to pick up our trail— Here," he said abruptly, tossing Lahr Docie's reins. "You fellers go ahead—"

"Where the hell d'you think *you're* goin'?" Lahr demanded.

"Go on," Cardigan said, "I'll catch up with you." Swinging down off his horse, he ran into the house.

Lahr swore, glaring after him, but kicked his horse into motion. The KC crew passed out of the yard.

They pulled up in a grove of scrub oak just beyond the north pasture and waited. Hennessy was all for pushing on, but Lahr said: "We'll wait. If that bastard's fixin' t' sell us out we better know it now."

Docie's look held contempt. "If he'd wanted to do that—"

"I don't want no lip outa *you!*" Lahr snarled; and Krailor said, "More likely he went back t' dig up that cash he done us out of."

Lahr sat silent, plainly turning it over. Then he shook his head. "Good part of it's in silver; he'd need a couple extra broncs if he was figurin' t' fetch that with him."

"Here he comes," Hennessy growled. And, when Kurt came up, "How come we don't hear them horses no more?"

"I put a lamp in the window," Kurt said with a grin. "It'll give us another mile's start, anyway, while that bunch is injunin' up on the place. They can't be sure you boys stopped an' they won't want t' miss me."

They rode steadily for a quarter of an hour, holding their horses to a ground-eating walk. The way angled upward in easy stages and Krailor laughed when they heard shots behind them. Grass carpeted these slopes and some of the earlier roughness fell out of the wind.

The country grew wilder, the upgrades steeper and the

grass petered out and left shale underfoot. The horses' hoofs slithered and clacked in it and Docie had to lean forward to stay in her saddle.

There was a ridge shoving up in front of them, a bare expanse of rock-studded slope which the moon made almost as bright as day. Lahr swung his horse toward it. Now and then from the sides of her eyes Docie had quick glimpses of trails running crosswise, and of great boulders which had fallen from the mountains and which now strewed the slopes like miniature houses.

It was a desolate region they were into now where nothing but cacti and rock abounded, some of the cactus towering forty feet high. They crossed the ridge and found another and higher one bulking before them with a thicket of squatting cedar at its base.

Cardigan's voice came up to her. "You smell anythin', Lahr?"

Lahr sniffed and looked back and shook his head.

"Well, keep your eyes skinned," Kurt said grimly. "The Phoenix road crosses this trail just beyond that next ridge."

They went on again, slowly, Lahr picking his way with more and more care. It was colder up here with a kind of dry stillness that made every sound seem uncommonly sharp.

Branches slapped at her face as they passed through the cedars, and then they were quartering up the steep slope, the horses slipping and sliding through the clattering talus. They struck the rim and climbed over and saw a whole world of timbered uplands before them, the black shapes of the nearest trees but a scant quarter mile ahead.

Cardigan passed her, spurring up beside Lahr, and they went on that way for a hundred yards and came out on a wagon-tracked road and stopped.

Cardigan held up a hand for silence. To their right the road, climbing up from Tucson, came out on the ridge in a tangle of juniper. To the left it followed the line of timber and was lost in the moonlit distance.

Twisting in the saddle, Cardigan sent a long look toward the right. Though she herself heard and saw nothing, it was plain to Docie that Kurt was disturbed. She saw him jerk a look at Lahr and saw Lahr's head dip. "Dust," Lahr murmured, and then she smelled it herself. It was very faint.

Cardigan threw another look at that tangle of juniper, then his glance went slowly over the road and picked at the black stand of trees beyond it. "More than one," he said softly. "Been through here in the last five minutes and, since they didn't use the road, they must have cut through the timber."

He said more and more thoughtfully, "If they're headin' the other way they came from town an' may be huntin' us. What's your idea, Curly? You reckon Frank's split up his posse figurin' we might do just what we have done?"

Hennessy said in a lather of impatience: "Fiddlin' round here ain't goin' t' solve nothin'. While we're settin' here jawin' them fellers at the ranch will be on their way up here—"

"So they'll be on their way up here," Cardigan said, "an' if this other bunch is part of 'em and we're trapped in between 'em it ain't goin' to be any picnic."

Lahr said, "I'm for turnin' left an' takin' the Phoenix road fer a spell. We'll make better time—"

"An' we'll be easier seen," Cardigan pointed out. "Besides, if it's part of Frank's posse, they'll expect us to do that. I got a hunch we better—"

He went suddenly still. Below them, in a south southeasterly direction, there came the sharp flat crack of a rifle.

Cardigan and Lahr exchanged glances. Before either man could speak there came a long high yell from above and to the left of them, and at once the night was filled with the crash of breaking brush as hard-ridden horses came plunging toward them through the timber.

"They've cut us off," Cardigan said. He grabbed Docie's reins and thrust them into her hands, and immediately swung the dun stallion, sending him into the road toward town and lifting him into a headlong gallop.

Flame in two places knifed out of the junipers and Lahr swept the thicket with a blast from his rifle; and then they were past, tearing down the white road. But, almost at once, Cardigan left it again, driving the big dun into the timber and up a narrow lane through the trees. Then he held up his hand and they stopped, grimly waiting, and saw two horse-men rush past on the road.

Hennessy started to lift up his reins but Cardigan reached out and stopped him. "Wait." They heard the men then who had been in the junipers; they were angling uphill through the trees, coming toward them; and then the sounds stopped and a six-shooter spoke three times very rapidly. Down on the road another gun answered and not fifty yards from Cardigan's crew Reagan's voice shouted: "They're up here some-place—in the timber!"

Lahr cursed under his breath and, from the road, the voice of Esparza's deputy, Hankins, sent a clear *How you know?* from the entrance to the lane.

"We heard 'em," the liveryman answered. "We've got them horse-stealin' bastards now. Spread out down there an' work this way."

Cardigan said in the quietest of voices: "Four men—could be five. Two in the timber, mebbe three on the road. What's it look like to you, Lahr?"

"Duck soup." Lahr grinned. "All we got t' do is foller those orders; them birds in the timber won't know us from their own crowd. We drift up t' them two an' shut their mouths. When them fellers from the road shove up, we drop 'em. Slick, quick an' easy."

Docie shuddered. She didn't see how Kurt could work with such a man, or how Lahr would much want to work with Kurt either after the trouble they'd had at the ranch this afternoon. Kurt was a fool to throw in with them again. . . .

Toward the road, but much nearer, she heard the hoofs of a horse crush fallen limbs, and she saw the dark blob of Kurt's head abruptly nod. "All right," he said quietly. "You take the far right of the line, Lahr. Hennessy an' Krailor will advance in the center an' me an' the girl will come up on the west—"

"Just a minute," Lahr growled, swinging round in the saddle. "You wouldn't be fixin' t' run out on us, would you?"

"How far do you think I would get runnin' out?"

"Not very damn far!"

"Let's go," Cardigan murmured, and swung off to the left, Docie following. She heard the others drift off and then their more cautious sounds were lost in the noise of the men from the road.

She kept watching for Cardigan to turn the dun's head up into the timber toward Reagan's position, but he kept heading west; and then she saw the moonlit road through the trees and knew that Lahr's suspicion had been right. Kurt had had no intention of joining in that slaughter; and suddenly she felt better than she had in a long while.

Cardigan stopped the dun just short of the road and waited for her to come up with him. She put a hand on his arm. "Thank you, Kurt."

He looked at her a moment. Snuffy let out a sigh and watched the road with his ears cocked. She couldn't make out Kurt's expression with his head turned that way, but she squeezed his arm.

He said, "We ought to—"

The crack of a rifle sheared off his words. It came from the direction of Reagan's position, and three further shots laid their explosions through the timber. One high, wild cry went into the night; and then a tremendous racket of gunfire broke loose and Docie heard the crash of running horses up there. Someone yelled, "Cardigan! Cardigan!" and Lahr's voice slammed through the uproar with a wilder and wilder fury.

"Come on!" Cardigan said, and spurred his dun stallion into the road, turning him up the road toward Phoenix, but soon letting him drop into a walk on the grade. They passed the juniper tangle and were cresting the rise when Cardigan reached out and grabbed her bay's bridle, pulling both horses up sharply. "Listen!"

But there was no need to listen. They could both hear it plainly, even above the fight in the timber. There was a pounding rush of hoofs on that road; like a roar of surf that sound ran toward them.

"Quick!" Cardigan cried, and swung the yellow horse crossways of the road, pulling her bay around with it. "We'll have to drop back down." He put his quirt in her hands. "Lay it on!" he said; and then they were pelting across the bare ridgetop, pushing their horses to the limit to get below the rim before those others should catch sight of them. But they were seen anyway. Docie heard three guns cry out in unison, one of those bullets whistling past her cheek.

They were below the rim then, their horses slipping and sliding dangerously as they went plunging down the rocky face of the slope. She could hear shod hoofs pound the hard ground above them and then they were plunging through the dark line of cedars, crashing through the low brush, and racing across another bare ridge.

"Swing left!" Cardigan yelled, and she swung with him into a narrow defile which the trees had concealed until this moment. The floor of this gulch was littered with rock and pitched steeply downward in an easterly direction between tree-masked walls. After five hundred feet it bent south again and then once again east and came out in a tiny deep-grassed basin about a thousand yards across.

Cardigan stopped and she pulled up beside him, hearing the pursuit roar across the bare ridge and dive into the cedar brakes, the sound of its progress afterward dying to a distance-dimmed rumor. She saw where the moon hung low in the south, seeing how the grayness of the eastern sky was commencing to show the ragged tops of mountains. It would soon be dawn, she thought with astonishment.

She looked at Cardigan, wishing it were lighter so she could make out the expression on his beard-stubbled cheeks. He must be terribly weary. She knew his wound must be giving him a lot of pain, too; and she marveled anew at his capacity for punishment.

She said, "That man, Krailor—he was with those men who robbed the Bisbee bank. He took care of their horses. He was the one who shot the man in the stage office."

Cardigan said, "I oughta be kicked, draggin' you into this thing," and sat a while, silent, staring into the south. "Funny," he said, "the way things . . ." and let the rest go.

He got out of his saddle and loosened the cinches; came around, helped her down, and then loosened hers. "I reckoned on gettin' through but it looks like now that was damn foolish figurin'. Like about all the rest of the things I've done."

"You mean . . . like sending for me?"

He stood a while thinking or, perhaps, just watching her. When he finally spoke it was to counter with a question. "Would you still of bought that ticket, knowin' what you know now?"

"I don't know," she said honestly. "Probably not."

He said, "I remember the first time I saw you. You were right when you told me I couldn't believe my luck." She saw the brief glint of his teeth, then he said: "Time t' go," and went over and retightened his cinches, then came back and retightened hers.

He gave her a hand to the saddle and his hand, going back, brushed across her bare knee. It brought his glance down at once and he stood absolutely still. She guessed he hadn't noticed before what the brush had done to her clothes. His head tipped up and she knew his eyes were searching her face. A kind of sigh welled out of him. He said: "I want you t' know I'm goddam sorry about everythin'."

He stood looking at her a moment longer and then went over to his horse and got into the saddle.

They crossed the basin at a steady walk and Docie was shocked to see how much nearer the day had come. Above the eastern mountains the sky was brightening rapidly. In almost no time at all the sun would be up, throwing its revealing light over all. She had a strong and unwelcome conviction Esparza's posse would not look such fools once the confusion of darkness had left the land.

Even as the thought took shape in her mind a sound of rifle fire threw up its clatter again from some place far below and a bit to the left of them; and Docie stopped with her eyes flown to Cardigan, hearing the echoes of this madness roll and break and fade through the hills.

Cardigan sat with his shoulders bowed, listening; and she tried to put herself in his place, but she could only think how it would be with her if she found herself being chased by a posse. Of course she *was* being chased, but it was Kurt they were after.

"Lahr," he said, and put his horse on the trail again.

"What are you going to do?"

"Keep runnin', I reckon."

"Wouldn't you have a better chance if I . . . if I weren't with you?"

"Probably," he said, without looking around.

"At least you don't have to be so blunt about it."

He looked around then and she could see his eyes. They were not the eyes she had remembered. "I don't have much talent for your kind of talk. You asked me a question. I answered it."

"Where are you going?" she asked, after a moment.

"I'm takin' you back to the ranch."

"But . . . but isn't that dangerous—for you, I mean?"

"Sure." A twisted grin streaked across his cheeks. "I want t' be a martyr an' fix things up so you can go back where you come from an' get this hand dealt over."

He spat at a pine and drew the rifle from its boot and gave her a look that was anything but flattering. "Now suppose you give your jaw a rest an' let me get in a little figurin'."

Trees were all about them and he rode with his eyes raking each patch of shadow. She could see the sun now where it touched the high crags and gilded the ramparts of the black eastern mountains. And, abruptly, he lifted a hand for quiet.

The report of fast traveling swelled out of the east to a sustained and rapid onrush of sound, passing loudly across some nearby corridor with a lifted voice saying sharply, "Try that left fork!" and the shod hoofs dropping at once to a whisper as though the mouth of some gulch had gobbled them.

"Esparza," Cardigan said, and leaned forward as though he might see beneath the down-drooping branches. Then he moved the dun on and she fell in behind again.

Almost immediately they were out of this wood and staring down the length of a shallow ravine that was half blocked with windfalls. Presently Cardigan stopped and sat eyeing the ground, and when she came up he pointed out the deep tracks. "Four of 'em. Here's where they crossed. Game's tightening up."

These hours in the saddle had left their mark on him. He looked older and leaner, much less sure of himself, and two days' growth of bristle blurred the line of his jaw.

She bit her lip and looked away and then looked back at him again. And color ran through her cheeks and she said, very low: "You don't have to take me back."

He didn't look round. He stared a while longer at the brush up ahead and then, as though satisfied, turned the dun into the trail out of which that fragment of the posse had just come. A rifle cracked once far above and to the left of them, that sound followed by a distant hallooing. Kurt said, "I'm goin' back anyway."

"But that's crazy!"

"I do a lot of crazy things."

"But *why?* What is there in it for you? I tried to get you to stay there in the first place and you wouldn't. You said—"

"I know what I said. You wanted me to stay there and face that posse an' I told you there was people that would ask nothin' better than for me to be caught with a bunch of cheap crooks."

"But I told you I'd tell—"

"An' I told you that posse would do its talkin' with rifles. You been hearin' 'em, ain't you? I don't know what fellers are with that bunch but there's bound to be some Lahr has turned against me that would like nothin' better than a chance t' cut me down."

"Then why go back now?"

Cardigan grinned without mirth. "A little matter of business. Lahr ain't the only one around can set traps. That slick son will be back an' when he comes I wanta be there."

"I guess I'm not very bright."

"You ain't no dumber than I was. Took me quite a spell to understand that feller. Not sure I do yet, but I *will*. He tied up with my bunch about a year ago. We'd been roundin' up unbranded horses up north, fetchin' 'em down here an' sellin' them for good money. You'd be plumb right t' call it crooked, though there wasn't no law against it then. It was just a plain case of take your own chances. If you got by with it, fine. If you didn't you got handed your come-uppance muy pronto."

The trail crossed a dry wash and came into a region of rocks and scrub oak. Cardigan seemed more to be putting his own mind in order than doing this talking for Docie's benefit.

"Lahr was right slick. I guess right from the first he knew what he wanted. There was a girl there in town had her cap set for him; I never give it much thought but it all adds up. He was after my spread, which is the biggest one round here in point of importance, rep an' stock quality. He must of seen from the start where his big risk was me; he had to figure some way to get me took care of if he ever was goin' t' git his hooks in KC. He had t' get rid of me—an' he sure done his best to.

"I can call t' mind now a whole passel of things I couldn't quite savvy when they was bein' dealt out t' me— that marshal, fer instance, an' this give-away horse. But I was playin' in luck an' not even the lyin' rumors he spread was enough in themselves t' pull me down. So he began buildin' up for a powdersmoke showdown; his lies might still help, an' the horse an' the marshal; but to make sure a posse would ride an' do the job for him he needed spilled blood an' a gutted safe.

"Soon's I took off huntin' you he turned wolf. He robbed two banks an' a stage carryin' money, killin' two guys an' the Bisbee marshal. He raided Amado an' drove stock out of my neighbors' back yards, worked over the brands and left the stuff runnin' around loose on my range. I don't know how he figured t' get loose when the crash come, but it's a cinch he had some sly way figured. An' he can still get away with the whole stinkin' business if I don't git back there t' stop him."

Docie rode a little way without speaking. Then she said, "But won't the posse . . . won't Esparza suspect—"

"He prob'ly will. But Frank's a square-shooter; he can't act without proof. An' he won't have no proof Lahr was anyplace round this business tonight. All Lahr needs is an alibi, an' a guy slick as him'll have five or six handy."

"Is that why you're so sure he'll come back to the ranch?"

"No. By my figurin' he would come back anyway. The money—cash an' currency—we took in from that stock we stole up north is still there in the house, an' he'd come back after that if for no other reason. Twenty thousan' dollars would take him quite a long ways."

23

LAST ACT

*I*T WAS a strange world of stone they were riding through now. Great blocks of rock, broken loose from the mountain flanks, lay all about them in weird assortment, the trail tortuously curving between and around them. The shod hoofs of their horses rang unconscionably loud though Kurt, if he noticed, seemed to give no mind to it. She guessed the pain of his wound might be at him again, or perhaps it was fatigue that pulled his broad shoulders down; or the both of them together. He had the rifle across his saddle again but he didn't seem to be doing much looking around.

She was bone weary herself and would be glad to be done with this endless riding. She hadn't been on a horse in five or six months and she dreaded to think how she would feel tomorrow; but, mostly, she just thought of Kurt and his problems and, very briefly, of her own. Her own after all, compared to his, were pretty simple. She could stay on in Tucson or go back to St. Louis.

But where could Kurt go? He didn't even seem to give a thought to that himself. All of Kurt's thoughts seemed to begin and end with Lahr; about half the time, she guessed, he even forgot that she was with him. And yet . . . that time that he had kissed her . . .

The crash of a rifle brought the chin off her chest. She saw Kurt sway wildly and go out of the saddle. Saw the roll of his body and the dust beat up round it; and the flame gouting out of his extended right hand. And then a scream, high and frightened, tore through all of that racket and she saw Kurt, up on his feet again, go zigzagging into those rocks on the right; heard his gun bang again and then his voice calling out to her.

She kneed her horse off the trail and in between two great rock slabs, hearing Snuffy, who had stopped, cautiously coming along behind her. Over against a bright patch of sunlight she saw Kurt bending over something that was hidden from her behind a three-foot rounded boulder. And, coming nearer, she saw the man.

He was propped with his back up against the rock. He had a derby on his head above a scared white face. The left leg of his rumpled store-bought trousers was pulled above the knee; there was a tourniquet about it and Kurt was bending over him doing something with a knife. Then she saw the dead snake, a big diamondback rattler with his head blown half off.

The man's eyes had a crazy half-glazed expression and great beads of sweat stood out on his face. He looked like some kind of traveling salesman; and then she saw with alarm the widening stain on Kurt's shirt.

"Take this gun," Kurt said, passing her a short-barreled pistol, "an' keep your eye on this guy while I try t' suck out that poison."

"But, Kurt!" she cried, beside herself, "don't you hear—"

"Yeah, I hear 'em. Some of this feller's playmates comin' down from above, I reckon. Heard the shots," he said, with a twisted grin. "But they wouldn't get here in time t' help him."

Bending down, he went to work on the leg. And, when he had finished and spat out the last trace of rattlesnake venom, the noise of the oncoming posse was a racketing noise of all too near sound.

"Get into your saddle, Docie," Kurt said; and, to the man: "What you done with your horse?"

"Shot down in a brush with some of your gang."

"Here? When?"

"None of your goddam business."

Kurt looked at him. "Well, thanks," he said, and swung into the saddle. "If you don't want t' spend the rest of your life here you better get out an' flag them boys down."

It seemed to Docie the posse might be right on their heels; but Kurt said no, it was the rocks made it sound that way. "We oughta make the ranch three-four minutes ahead of 'em —barrin' accidents."

They rode for ten minutes and came out of the rocks on a dry drab carpet of drought-stricken grass. Far off to the south she saw the trees and log buildings of Cardigan's ranch.

"You ought to let me take care of that—"

"Later," Kurt said. "Hell—don't worry about me."

She looked back after a while but the posse still hadn't come into sight. She told Kurt. He nodded. "We been savin' our horses a lot more than they have. But Frank Esparza's no fool. They'll be along in time t'—"

"They're comin' now!"

Cardigan looked back over his shoulder. "Yeah. That's Frank, all right. Looks like the Flowerpot boss an' Joe Nettleton with him. We got three-quarters of a mile on 'em an' double that t' go. We'll make it—"

"But you can't stop now or they'll catch you!"

"I'll be stoppin'."

She looked at him worriedly. "But—"

"Some things means more to me than gittin' away, I reckon."

He let the big dun out another half notch and Docie gave up trying to talk to him. The wind plucked the words straight out of her mouth like chaff from a threshing. Her bay horse was game but he was tiring fast; he lacked considerable of being the horse Kurt was riding.

She looked back again and saw they were gaining. The men with Esparza were flogging their horses at every jump but the gap kept widening. She felt a little encouraged. Perhaps after all—

Cardigan ripped out a curse.

She saw him staring toward the ranch. And then she saw what had caught his attention, and her own eyes widened with a dawning horror. About three hundred yards this side of the buildings a man on horseback was dragging a burning something across the range at a headlong gallop, and in a great arc behind him the dry prairie grass was leaping into flame.

The sharp glitter of anger was in Cardigan's eyes, of an anger more terrible than any she had seen, and all the bones of his face stood out; she knew then he would kill Curly Lahr if he could. It was a wildness in him, the yeastiness of an affronted pride. He had enjoyed a certain prestige in this country, a reputation for toughness and shrewdness; he'd been Lord of the Hills—a bad man with a gun. And Lahr, by his acts, had torn this to shreds.

These things she read in Cardigan's look. And then he was gone in a swirl of dust, seeming to forget what horse was under him. Consumed by his hate, by his need for revenge, he was spurring the big dun without mercy, driving him straight at that brightening blaze.

She called on the wearying bay for more speed, wondering if the whole range were threatened; wondering, too, why Lahr had set this fire which must surely wipe out everything he had schemed for. If he'd planned, as Kurt thought, on bluffing this through, what had ever possessed him—

And then, of her knowledge, the answer came to her. Lahr had naturally thought to be rid of Kurt as a culmination to Esparza's visit. It must have come as a terrible shock to the man to have looked up and seen Kurt Cardigan coming across these flats with the posse behind him.

That was it—Lahr had panicked. Had been filled with a sudden overpowering fright on beholding Cardigan riding toward him. She had seen Kurt put that fear into men; into Lahr himself and into Shiloh Frayne. Curly Lahr cared for life even more than he cared for the fruits of his treachery and, abandoning all, he had set this fire in the desperate hope that it might cut Kurt off, might hold him back until Lahr could hide his trail and get out of the country.

She beat her heels against the bay's heaving sides, sending him tearing after Kurt's stallion, her dilated eyes glued to Cardigan's shape. Smoke was commencing to roll up now as the burning grass sucked wind like a draft. Fifty yards from the yellow-red glow she could hear the rising roar of the flames; and her heart almost stopped when she saw Jubal Jo rearing up before them. But Kurt fought him down with an iron hand and they whirled to the left, plunging recklessly on, trying to find some way past that wall of flame.

Docie turned the bay and gained thirty yards, felt him lift to the call of the singing quirt. But he was failing fast. She could feel the great muscles quivering under her, could see the slow fall of that gallant head; only his fighting heart kept them going. But she dared not stop here—to stop here was death; they must get beyond reach of these ravening flames.

Her smarting eyes were filled with tears from the smoke and sometimes now she couldn't see Kurt at all. But always she could hear the yellow stallion's hoofs, even through the roar of the flames she could hear them—even above the groaning breath of the bay.

She felt the bay falter, felt the changing rhythm of his pace —felt him stumble. She stood in the stirrups, held him up with main strength; heard him cough. The smoke in great billowing gusts was all about them, recurringly pierced by the brief orange tridents of crackling flame that winked and danced and fluttered. And again the bay faltered; and she knew, this time, by his staggering strides that the end was at hand. And then—

Oh, blessed relief! Amazing, incredulous—they were out of the smoke and beyond the fire's reach in a splendid great open of hoof-tracked dust where nothing at all grew to give the fire purchase. Twenty yards the bay ran and then he started to fold. She kicked free of the stirrups and struck heavily, rolling.

But the deep dust cushioned her fall and she got unsteadily onto her feet and, because someway it seemed the thing to do, began slapping the burned spots out of her dress. When she was satisfied there were no live sparks on her, she looked toward where she judged the ranch to be, but a burned-over hogback cut off her view. She heard no horses, no blast of gunfire. She guessed Kurt was trying to track down Curly Lahr.

She saw now that she was in a kind of depression that looked to have been made by the hoofs of penned stock. Climbing to higher ground she found her view increased considerably, though she still couldn't see whether or not the ranch were burning—the buildings, that is. Out on the flats of the north pasture great clouds of dark smoke showed the fire was still marching inexorably toward the foothills and she guessed it would not stop before it reached that boulder basin.

Turning round she saw that in the opposite direction, which was dead against the wind, the fire had burned freakishly, skirting the shallow ravine over there, yet leaping a creek to go tearing across a stretch of high ground and then, balked by a forty-foot ledge of buff sandstone, dipping east through a thicket of chaparral. That arm of the fire was now creeping toward a flimsy shed and pine board shanty some thousand yards to the south of her.

And then she saw Cardigan.

He was on his yellow horse, sitting straight-legged in the saddle and moving at a snail's pace across the smoking high ground south of the ravine and west of the creek beyond it. He had his rifle across the pommel so, presumably, he had not yet found the man he was hunting.

If he thought to find Lahr in this neighborhood—and it was obvious to her that he was working back this way—he must already have looked to the south and west, the most natural directions for Lahr to have run. This meant Kurt had some-

way cut the man off and prevented the getaway Lahr's panic
had prompted. Therefore Lahr must have taken to cover.

She felt suddenly afraid for Kurt on that ridgetop. He
seemed very tall limned that way against the sky and the
stringers of smoke curling up from burned timber. He had
his hat shoved back and, on that yellow horse, the sun turned
the edges of his hair a bright gold.

So alone he looked—was it pride that made him expose
himself so? Did he think it the quickest means to his purpose? She wanted to cry out *Get off that ridge!* but she dared
make no sound or move which might even for an instant
divert his attention.

She tried to think where Lahr might hide if he were
round here, and her glance sped at once to the shed and
board shanty. They were down in that hollow to the east
of the creek, and the fire working down that side of the creek
was less than a hundred yards from them now. If the man
were there he'd have to pick up soon. Perhaps that place was
out of range for a rifle or, if someway Kurt had cut him off
from his horse, perhaps he had no rifle but only a belt gun.

And then she saw why it was Kurt didn't look toward that
place. He was working the west side of the ridge just above
the ravine; the shed and the shanty would not be in his vision
until he rounded the rock strewn base of the slope.

And then she saw Lahr.

He was in the ravine, fifty feet below Kurt, well concealed
among the vine-covered branches of a windfall. But now the
sound of the dun stallion's nearness had drawn his lank shape
very carefully erect; and he was crouched, bending forward,
with his outstretched arm along the gray barked trunk. It
was the sunlight glinting off the barrel of his pistol which
had shown her where he was.

Even as she spied him a snake's head of flame winked
wickedly upward from the snout of that pistol. She saw
Cardigan flinch. She saw the shine of his teeth as he lifted the
rifle and coolly fitted the butt to his shoulder. Snuffy stood like
a rock. She saw Cardigan's lips move but all she could hear
was the trip-hammer pounding of Lahr's flaming pistol. But

the man's nerves were ragged, he was in a panic of haste, firing wildly and furiously as fast as he could trigger.

The flat crack of Kurt's rifle came through that sound cleanly.

Lahr's head tipped back and, with his mouth stretched wide, his arm slipped slowly off the bole's gray bark. Docie didn't see him fall. Some compulsion stronger than anything in her had turned her startled eyes toward the pine board shack.

The breath caught in her throat. The fire had reached its east corner but it wasn't that inferno of flame that blanched her cheeks. Aghast she was staring at the white-gowned figure that on hands and knees was crawling from the now open door.

Docie screamed, and pointed.

Cardigan, across the ravine, took one look. He lifted the big dun on hind legs and whirled him, sent him recklessly plunging across the shale littered slope. Down the creek side he flashed at a hard pounding run. She saw Cardigan lift him and put him across it—saw the stallion dive, squealing, between blazing trees and slide into the dooryard on locked, sliding heels.

Before he stopped Kurt was out of the saddle, tearing the rolled slicker away from his cantle. Docie saw him run forward, slicker over his shoulders, to where the girl lay in a crumpled white heap not ten feet from the flames. Fire enveloped the shanty; in a gust of bright sparks flame swirled from the doorway and curled over Kurt as he stooped, gently rolling the unconscious girl in his slicker.

She saw the girl's red hair flying loose and wild as he gathered her up in his arms and straightened; saw him bend again—holding the girl with one arm and a knee—and scoop the hair into his hat, putting it on her. Then he turned, still bent, using his body to shield her, and carefully moved toward his horse.

Docie couldn't help it. She screamed again when she saw the blazing tree fall square across Kurt's path. A volcano of sparks and flaming branches obscured him; then she saw him again, still holding the girl, trapped away from his horse by the tree's blazing length.

Her heart almost failed when she saw Snuffy bolt.

She heard Cardigan whistle; heard him whistle again and saw the big dun stop and look back uncertainly; heard him whinny and snort. Saw him shake himself violently. Even from here she could see his shape tremble, could see the wild roll of his terrified eyes.

Kurt whistled again and Snuffy pawed at the ground. He took a few nervous steps and stopped, shaking all over. She could see how he watched Kurt, though; and then, with head held so as to keep up the reins, he went reluctantly toward him, whinnying softly. Step by step he moved nearer, terribly frightened and nervous but with his trust in Kurt bringing him always in closer, until he stood just across the burning tree from his master. Kurt fought his way across it with the unconscious girl held aloft in his arms and, with clothes still smoking, got into the saddle.

They were waiting for him when he came out of the flames.

"Some hoss," Collquist said—he was the owner of Flower-pot. And Rickven, with tears streaming down his stubbled cheeks, took the girl from his arms. Top Hat Charlie nodded.

"Well," Cardigan said, looking down at Esparza, "let's get it over with."

"No hurry," Frank said. "She bad hurt?"

"I think she'll make it, all right. If there's anythin' left of my place—"

"Main house an' cook-shack."

"Better take her up there then. My woman'll help."

Esparza looked briefly at Docie and nodded. "I got your note—the one you left on the table."

Cardigan scrubbed a hand across his chin, leaving another streak of soot in its wake and smearing one that was already there. He let out a sigh. "You'll find the cash on a coupla packed horses I tied out in the brush about a mile south of here." He licked his cracked lips and said: "All of it."

"So he was all set to run, eh?"

Cardigan shrugged.

Docie touched Frank Esparza on the arm and said shyly, "I'd like to say a few words, if you'll let me. I know Kurt's too proud to speak up for himself—he thinks a man ought to stand or fall by his actions; but it seems to me a man's actions could be misunderstood—he misunderstood Lahr till it just about ruined him. I want you to know that man Lahr was a scoundrel!"

"I've suspected as much," Esparza told her gravely.

"I can prove it, too," Docie said emphatically. "I was at the stage station when the Bisbee bank was robbed, and Lahr was the leader—I saw him shoot that marshal; and our crew was in it with him. Jupe Krailor didn't even have a mask on; and I know Lahr was the leader because his hat came off when they were making their getaway and I saw his green eyes and red hair! I think he was the leader of those night-riders too; we've got misbranded horses all over our range."

No one stared any harder than Kurt, for all he was so weary he wasn't catching half of it.

"Kurt and me," Docie said. "were going to round them up—"

"We'll take care of that, ma'am—"

"Well that will surely be a help, short-handed like we are. Kurt fired the whole crew, but they came through here last night with a big bunch of horses—"

"Yeah. We know about that."

"Did you know Kurt and me were trying to track them down?"

"We kind of suspected as much," Espraza nodded. "That Lahr was a pretty bad actor. Did you know he wrote Sollantsy here—Sollantsy's a rep for the Tri-States cattle crowd— that your husband was riding a dun called Jubal Jo that was stolen from a rancher at Big Timber, Montana?"

Here it comes, Kurt thought; and was too pooped to give a damn, though it had kind of halfway made him mad to hear Docie putting her oar in that way—who the hell did she think she was kidding! And that puking dude—imagine that guy being a Tri-States range dick!

Docie said, "I'm not a bit surprised. You should have heard some of the lies he told my husband."

The marshal nodded. "Just for the sake of the record though, Sam, do you reckon this could be the horse Lahr was jawin' about?"

Cardigan saw the dude stepping forward. He had a hard time bringing the guy's face into focus. To hell with him, he thought, and wished to Christ they would hurry and get it over.

"You mean this nag?" the dude said with a sneer. "Jubal Jo was a *horse*—not a goddam pony!"

You could have knocked Cardigan's eyes off his cheeks with a stick. It was the damnedest thing he had ever heard tell of; yet there the guy was, tramping off with Joe Nettleton, Hankins and some other birds, heading for their saddles. Hell, it must be Docie, he thought, plumb astounded. She seemed to have pulled the wool over everyone!

"Guess we better be shovin' along," Frank was saying; and the next thing he knew there he was alone with Docie. She looked kind of scared, and well she had a right to be. "I never could stand a lyin' woman," he told her, "but if you figure you could reform I reckon we better git hitched up." A grin cut across his tough face, changing it. "I sure wouldn't want Frank thinkin' he'd been deceived!"

EN